USA *Today* BESTSELLING AUTHOR
Dale Mayer

TERKEL'S TEAM SERIES
CALUM'S CONTACT

BOOK 04

CALUM'S CONTACT: TERKEL'S TEAM, BOOK 4
Dale Mayer
Valley Publishing Ltd.

ISBN-13: 978-1-773365-18-3
Print Edition

Books in This Series:

Damon's Deal, Book 1

Wade's War, Book 2

Gage's Goal, Book 3

Calum's Contact, Book 4

Rick's Road, Book 5

About This Book

Welcome to a brand-new series from *USA Today* best-selling author Dale Mayer, where dark-ops SEALs have special senses and skills, needed to solve intrigue, betrayal, and … murder. A series with all the elements you've come to love, plus so much more, … including psychics!

As his career path led him into more and more danger, Calum made a decision to keep his family safe, even if it meant he would be alone in the world. But when his wife and son are kidnapped and dumped almost into his very own secret headquarters, Calum knows his safeguards haven't been enough.

Mariana didn't like Calum's decision from years ago but finally understood after her and her son are rescued from kidnappers, and she saw the dangerous level of his work. However, having him once again in her life, their family whole again, she's not willing to let him go. Not this time. If the danger would continue, … surely they were safer at his side.

Calum's abilities at an all-time low, his friends and fellow teammates injured and struggling, Calum knows he must be there for the team. Yet protecting his family comes first. But, if they don't get to the bottom of the chaos that's his current life, … no one is safe.

Sign up to be notified of all Dale's releases here!

https://smarturl.it/DaleNews

PROLOGUE

CALUM LANCASHIRE WALKED unsteadily forward, as he entered the temporary headquarters for Terk's team here in Manchester, England. Terk was here, giving freely of his energy, and, with every step that Calum took, he was getting stronger. He was using a cane, something that he'd never used in his life, and it was hard—damn hard, in fact. It was awkward and debilitating, but, hey, he was finally upright. Nothing worse than not being on his feet. He smiled at Terk. "Thank you."

"For what?" Terk asked.

"For keeping me alive, for one. For keeping Mariana alive, for two. And for saving my kid."

"For that, you're very welcome," Terk replied. "We have a lot to catch up on. You're way behind on the news."

"Where are they?"

"They're down the hall here just a bit," he stated. "Can you make it?"

"Of course I'll make it." When they opened the door, Cal heard a gasp, and he stepped inside. There was Mariana, standing beside a double bed that contained his son, four-year-old Little Calum. Cal opened his arms, and Mariana raced forward.

"I'll leave you three alone. Cal, we'll meet up later," Terk said, turning to leave.

After he left the room, but still in the hallway as he could be heard talking to someone, Mariana whispered to her husband, "I didn't know. I'm sorry. I just didn't know."

"I got it," he murmured. "I tried to tell you."

"And now I get it." She shook her head. "It was terrible, absolutely terrible, but we're safe, and now I have you back." She squeezed him hard.

He held her close, his face buried in her beautiful soft blond hair. She always smelled like the scent of roses, and yet she swore she never used any perfume. Maybe it was a whiff of her shampoo? He didn't know, but it was stunning, and it brought back so many memories that the tears choked the back of his throat. "I'm so glad you're safe," he whispered, "and I'm so damn sorry that you and our son got caught up in this nightmare."

She shook her head. "It's fine," she said quietly. "I get it. I mean, I really do understand now."

He shook his head. "You shouldn't have to *get it.*" He groaned. "At least they didn't hurt you two, thank God."

"No, but Little Calum is quite traumatized," she noted, "and I've had a hard time getting him to sleep."

"We'll find a safe place for you two, until this is over."

She pulled back ever-so-slightly, then looked up at him. "The kidnappers did mention a name. Rulrul," she murmured. "I don't know who that is but—"

At that, Terk stepped forward. "What, do you mean, *Rulrul?* What did they say?"

"Something like, 'Rulrul won't like this. He doesn't like involving kids or women.' But apparently it was a necessary tactic that they felt they had to employ."

"Now that's interesting," Terk replied. "Did you hear a last name or anything about a location?"

"Something to do with overseas, I think. I thought he meant Asia, but I don't really know."

"Did they say anything about the government? Or anything about being paid?"

"I overheard all kinds of bits and pieces," she noted. "It's obvious that they didn't worry about whether I heard or not," she murmured, "but it was pretty rough to make out words."

"Take your time. If you remember something later, no matter how insignificant, let us know," Terk replied. "I'm glad you remembered the name Rulrul."

"I only wish I had more, but I'm not sure that does any good."

"It does. Believe me. All intel does." Terk gave her a bright smile.

She held herself close against Cal.

He just wanted to hold her and to squeeze her tight. He dropped a kiss on her forehead. "I promise we'll get to the bottom of this," he told her, "and nobody will hurt Little Calum anymore. I'm so sorry."

She looked up at him, smiled, and murmured, "I know, and you aren't to blame. And maybe it's better in a way because now I understand why you walked away. I knew that you were concerned about danger to us, but I underestimated what that really meant and never expected to have it so forcibly shown to me."

"And it shouldn't have been," he snapped in a rough voice. Then he looked over at Terk.

She shook her head. "It's not Terk's fault."

"No, it's not," Calum said, "but you can bet we're all after answers. Real and final answers."

She stopped a moment, then smiled. "*Sean.*"

Both men looked at her, with quizzical expressions.

"Sean," she repeated. "One of the men they were talking with was Sean."

"Any idea in what capacity?" Terk asked.

"No, but I think he was the one who said something about Calum won't be happy."

"So, Rulrul won't be happy, and Calum won't be happy."

"I think Sean is the one who arranged for us to get picked up," she murmured. "I could be wrong though. … I don't really know. It was mentioned just in passing, as they were leaving, and one of the guys was speaking to the other one. The one guy said, 'Sean, this is your deal.' So I presumed the other guy was Sean. He laughed and said, 'Yeah, old Calum won't be happy with me.' Oh wait." She stopped, then looked at the two men. "Then Sean said something about it being a damn fine time for it. Something like, 'I've been waiting forever.' Does any of that make sense?"

At that, Calum stiffened and pulled her tightly into his arms again, holding her close. He looked at Terk over the top of her head. "That can't be Sean Calvert, can it?"

"I suggest we find out," Terk stated quietly. "Sean has been after you for a long time."

She pulled back, looked up at her husband.

He faced her and explained, "His life is a mess, and he's always blamed me for it. It could explain him grabbing you and our son."

"Did you do something to him?" she asked.

He immediately shook his head. "No, but a guy like that is just looking for excuses. He's glommed onto me as his enemy, and that's all he cared about. We were on friendly terms at one time."

4

She winced. "I'm sorry. That sounds pretty rough. For you and him."

"It was very rough for him apparently," Calum noted. "I've received threats from him over the years, and I've told him several times that I had nothing to do with his problems."

"But, like you said, he doesn't want to listen."

"Right, he doesn't want to listen at all," he added. "And obviously he has let that hate boil over to something completely out of hand, and he's not prepared to even consider the truth anymore."

"No." She shook her head. "Yet he sounded normal, looked normal, if *normal* is a term applied here."

He gave her a description of a man about five-eleven, with curly blond hair and a suntan, like a surfer.

She nodded slowly. "Yeah, exactly."

"Good," he confirmed, "at least now I know who it is. This time we'll have a meet-up that only one of us will walk away from."

"Then it damn well better be you," she cried out.

"I didn't come this far to lose you and Little Calum now." He smiled. "I worked really hard to survive that blast, and I have no intention of you losing me either, but I do intend to stop somebody who has such a hate-on for me that he'll continue to be a threat to us." He paused. "This is well past the point of normal behavior, and I had nothing to do with everything that's gone wrong in his life," he murmured. "It's well past time for him to understand it." And, with that, he leaned over, kissed her gently. "Besides, I have to keep you guys safe. And I'll do whatever it takes."

She threw her arms around him. "I know you will. You're not to blame for any of this, but please don't do anything stupid."

"I won't do anything stupid." Yet he felt his own temper still simmering. "But you can sure as hell bet that I won't let myself off as easily as you let me off."

She winced. "I knew you would take it the wrong way, if I told you anything."

"It doesn't matter," he replied. "We're at the point in time now where there's literally no going back. We have to get to the bottom of everything and stop this, Sean included. We've had a ton of our people attacked, and some didn't survive," he added quietly. "We all have families, and we all want to make sure everything's good."

"I get it," she agreed. "So go off and do your thing."

He smiled. "I wanted to just stay here and be with you for a little bit." But he caught sight of Terk, who shook his head.

"As much as that would be nice," Terk said, "it's not to be. We'll bring you up to date, and we need to hunt down Sean, before he causes any more trouble." And, with that, Terk left, clearly expecting Calum to follow.

The thing was, he would. Terk had been there for Calum every step of the way, and Cal would be there for Terk now. All Calum had to do was make sure that his team hunted down Sean and took out these assholes. And then go back after the other members of his team who were still comatose. Calum would do what he could to help pull them back out, just as Terk had pulled Cal out.

It was a terrible half-living state to be in, particularly for those with their kinds of abilities, used to pushing their bodies and their minds to the fullest extent, all in the protection of others. He kissed his wife gently once more. "I'll be back in a little bit."

She smiled, then nodded. "Go on. I know you have to, and it's fine. Just make sure you come home at the end of the day." And, with that, she stepped back and gave him a tentative wave. He walked over and kissed the sleeping child on the forehead, whispering in his ear. Then Cal headed out to follow Terk.

CHAPTER 1

C ALUM HATED THE fact that Mariana and his son were here. Yet he wanted to clutch the two of them close and never let them go.

He adored her, for God's sake, but a lot was going on. The fact that she was here to be with him was amazing, and he wanted every moment he could get with her, but the fact that she had been kidnapped, put in a lethal situation, only proved he'd been right to leave them behind so many years ago. He didn't want his family in jeopardy for another second because of the work Cal did, because of these assholes that Terk's team encountered too often, and everything that had happened recently was driving him mad.

He wanted a target to look for, someone he could blame, and a solution he could work toward, but, at the moment, just nothing fell in place, with no way to get anywhere closer to Sean and the guys that had blown up Terk's team.

Terk obviously understood what the hell Cal was going through, as he looked over at Calum. "We can't have you going on too many road trips," he murmured. "We must keep everybody here safe, but have you done any energy sessions to see if anybody out of Iran is still alive?"

Calum frowned. "Back to Iran? I thought we were discussing Sean Calvert."

"We are," Terk agreed, "but I need you to keep an eye

on Iran as well. It keeps popping up all over our intel."

Cal frowned. "*Huh.* I was pretty sure that was a done deal."

"We all were pretty sure it was a done deal," Terk noted, "but it doesn't look like it is."

"That's not good," he replied. "That was a major op for many reasons."

"I know." Terk nodded. "It makes me sick to think that we may have missed one person, and that mistake could end up costing us our lives."

"You mean, like it hasn't already cost us?" Calum stated, half bitterly.

"I get that you're upset about Mariana," he murmured. "I wasn't even aware that you were still together."

"I know"—he shrugged—"I basically kept them out of everything."

"And that's your prerogative," Terk noted. "We don't have to share all our personal and private information."

"No, we don't," Calum agreed, "but I do know how much difference it makes to the team as a whole if we aren't keeping secrets."

"Now that's true." Terk gave him a half smile.

"Damon filled me in on Celia."

At that, Terk's smile fell away, and he gave a clipped nod. "And we have no idea what the hell happened there either."

"But we will," he promised.

Terk once again stared at him. "We will. I was just hoping that it wasn't even part of the equation."

"Of course not," Calum stated. "I do think that you were planning to go to Texas, where she was dumped, says something."

"And what about that she's carrying my child?" he asked bitterly.

At that, Calum hesitated, then asked, "You're sure?"

"As sure as I can be without a DNA test," Terk replied, his voice low.

"Of course," Calum acknowledged, "and that's what they're counting on, isn't it? That you would know, with our particular skills, and that you would go there and save her."

"Well, it's not that we don't do that on a regular basis," Terk replied, "which means they also know all about us in every way." He shrugged. "Which I was assuming to begin with. So somebody has been tapping our lines or somebody inside the department has been passing over information, whether knowingly or not." He shook his head. "Bob was one of the defense department guys, and they took him out at the same time as the attacks on the rest of us."

"Weeding us out to focus on something more tangible, I suppose," Calum noted. "Last I heard, Sean was in the Netherlands." He looked at Terk. "If too many of us gather here, we'll draw attention."

"I know," Terk stated. "We're trying to find another location."

"Good," he noted. "With all of us in one corner like this, if we get taken out, it'll take all of us out."

"Again, I know," Terk muttered. "We're still looking at options."

"There aren't very many buildings that can shield our energy usage, and we need that to give us an additional layer of security, especially now that we have family left behind, when we go on ops." Calum sighed. "I don't suppose you want me to physically head to the Netherlands to track down Sean, especially not alone."

"No, I don't want you going, especially not alone. With half of us still down, I need you to do a little remote viewing first, see if you can confirm anything at all from Iran."

"I can do that now." Calum looked around. "Do we have a room or a secure place where we can do our energy work?"

"Yeah." Terk nodded. "I have two rooms that I have been working in."

"Okay, let me take a look at them." With that, they walked out of the main computer area and headed down to where Terk did his special work. "This might work," Calum noted, as he stood in the first room. "Interesting noise barriers."

"I know, but we don't have a whole lot of options."

"We never do," Cal muttered. "Okay, leave me alone here for a little bit, and I'll see if I can make anything activate."

"And remember. It's always about not getting tracked." Terk's tone was bitter.

Calum was a bit offended that Terk felt he had to tell him that.

Terk immediately added, "No offense meant. However, after the blast, everyone's skills have taken a hit. So I'd rather say something twice than not mention something that may have been wiped out of our memory banks by that attack."

Cal slowly nodded. "I know. The stakes have never been higher, ... not when my family is now here." He frowned. "This isn't a great place for a kid."

"Of course not." Terk backed away, as if to assess the damage he had done with the careless statement he had made. "We won't keep you and your family here for very long."

"Set up another safe house, and we'll move the family members over there."

"Not alone, no way," Terk ordered.

"Then give us half of what you've got here, … like maybe Wade and I move," he suggested quietly. "It would also ease some of the stress and congestion."

"Everything is possible, Calum. It's been an adjustment. Each time one of you came back to us, someone you loved came with you. Our family is slowly growing. I'll talk to the others. In the meantime, you go do your thing and check out Iran."

And, with that, Terk walked out, leaving Calum alone in the room, where he had absolutely no idea if he could pick up anything or not. Not only was he drained, exhausted, and damaged, he was also highly stressed. Not a very good situation when it came to energy work, considering what he wanted to accomplish here, with his remote viewing of Iran. When stressed, this kind of work was damn near impossible.

Maybe that was the overall intent of the attack and then the kidnapping. Maybe the enemy was looking to take out his family. These assholes had to figure initially that Calum could never function on this level again with the physical and psychic trauma he had sustained in the blast. Then to kidnap his family? That emotional trauma could end him. Those thoughts made him even more determined to get back out there and to get to the bottom of all this BS. He wanted so badly to get these guys for what they'd done to him, to his team, to his family.

He closed his eyes, settled into his normal position, and tried to destress and decentralize the voices in his head. He could only travel on the ethers like this if 100 percent relaxed and in total control of his emotions. And, even though it was hard, he tried slowing down his breathing. *One, ... two, ... three, the sun, the moon, the truth.*

He had picked up the phrase while training with Terk, and it had stayed with Cal. He could already feel himself tensing and worrying about Mariana. *Not now.* Instantly he pulled back and refocused. And, with the mantra ringing in his head, his vision slowly started to expand; it was working. With an enormous effort, he became a part of the soul of the world. He was soaring.

He looked down at their temporary headquarters. Little Calum was asleep still and curled up in his mom's lap. Calum saw them as he traveled, light on the air, through the same building that he was sitting in. It helped him to take a minute to orient himself and to mark his physical location, so he could return to these coordinates safely.

He headed out to the main computer room, where everybody sat, working—including Tasha, Sophia, and Lorelei. Some were talking to sort out the pertinent information; others focused on different tasks, but basically everybody minded their own part of this business and continued on, pushing to the common goal. A lot to be said for that. He didn't want to leave this atmosphere if he didn't have to. But, no doubt, if something went wrong with one of them, it could seriously affect all of them, every single one. And that was something that Calum couldn't handle. They'd already lost so much.

And that just blew him away because it showed the enemy's intel at a level that Cal didn't even want to think about. It meant people knowing what they were doing, when they were doing it, and how. These were people with an agenda— intent on taking down Terk's team.

Once again, Cal tried to empty his mind of his worries,

but it was hard. Pushing aside the pain in his chest, he finally stepped away from the whole mess and went back to his happy place, watching his Mariana with his son. Even as he watched her, she closed her eyes and gently tried to rest. He reached out mentally to her. *Just rest. We're all here, and we'll look after you.*

Her eyes flew open, and she sat upright. Stunned, he watched, as she looked around, frowning.

Had she heard him? That would be unusual and probably not a good thing in his line of work—although he wouldn't mind if they had that level of communication in their personal lives. He had always thought that, when he found the perfect partner for him, she could do the same things he was doing, but how many people in the world did this energy work? Not that he was an egotist by any means, but the type of work he did had taken a lot of training, a lot of time invested. Yet, here on the ethers, it seemed like everything was almost timeless.

He murmured again in her head, *I'm here. Just relax. Go to sleep and rest. Little Calum will be up soon, and you'll need to look after him.*

She frowned, then shifted her position and laid back down again, looking around the room, as if uncertain what to do.

He immediately sent what was the equivalent of a warm hug. She smiled, pulled the blankets up to her shoulders, and snuggled in. With her calm and somewhat happy, he then branched out farther, outside of the building, checking out the defenses in place.

Damon and Wade had both put up energy barriers that would be hard to cross, unless someone truly knew and had the kind of skills that his team had. He was proud of the team, damn proud, and they'd done incredible work for the safety of the American people. But nobody knew how their own government had fired them, and that fact made being in this position hurt so much more.

He knew that some of the others on Terk's team thought that the US government had been cleaning up, after closing down Terk's special department, making sure it was closed permanently. Cal wasn't so sure it was that simple.

They lived in a world of deception and betrayal, and too many people could have had access to their files. He was guessing here, conjuring up threads to follow, but it was possible that somebody—who shouldn't have had access— had sold personal info regarding Terk's team to the unknown enemy. And the fact that Mariana was here too said an awful lot about the team's personal files being exposed somehow and what other people knew.

Not just their enemies but their families too. Knowing was one thing, but whether they understood what they knew was a whole different story.

That Mariana was here and potentially part of the group now meant that the chances were very likely that Mariana had been told what the team does, but there was also a damn good chance that she only knew a little bit of it and not all of it. Did any of them even know all of it? Each of the guys had differing skill sets. Cal didn't know much about what his buddies could do, any more than they understood Cal's gifts.

He was straining hard now to remain on the ethers, especially while distracted like this.

Well, Terk knew everything about every guy on his team. This was his deal, his project. It had all been Terk's idea; he had brought this dream team into fruition, and he had trained them all. The fact that he'd even found them was something else. Calum often still wondered about that because it's not as if Terk could just place a want ad for people like them.

Terk had searched them out, had hunted them down, had sorted them, and had brought them on board. Of course it also helped to be somebody who had the same kind of skills that Calum had. Before that, all anyone knew, and all the military knew, was that Calum had a strong intuition. It had taken a lot of time and training on the part of Terk to help Cal realize his potential, to focus on it, to embrace it, to enhance it, becoming so much more than what it had been.

Calum wasn't prepared to let go of that either, not at this stage. He didn't know whether any of his team would be interested or not in forming up as an independent team, a non-governmental entity, but Cal suspected they would. They could still do so much good in the world, and, at the same time, they should be allowed to do it. However, it didn't look like the US government was prepared to let them. In which case, governmental decisions had been made, and obviously they'd come off on the wrong side of that decision-making.

Terk's team was dangerous, according to the government, and maybe they were. Maybe it was true. Calum wasn't so sure. They'd only ever worked for the US government, helping their fellow man. But fear of the unknown—and Terk's team was full of unknowns—makes people do all kinds of crazy things, and maybe that's what happened.

But where did Terk's team go from here? How did they go from here? That was, … well, … the million-dollar question, and it was something Calum wasn't prepared to contemplate.

Gathering up his energy, he made a swoop into his target coordinates in Iran and homed in on his view outside of the lone building, merging into the sand, as both were the same color. He looked around and saw from his aerial viewpoint just what was here. It was interesting that he didn't see a whole lot, and, of course, that was intentional. The goal was to be invisible to drones, so as not to pick up any activity either, since, of course, drones were out there.

And there was energy activity. Cal could sense it, but he didn't know who was watching the ethers. Calum had limitations, and, if Wade had his abilities back at full speed, he may see more. Calum closed his eyes and thought back to where he'd been in Iran and about the mission they'd recently completed there.

Almost instantly he stared at the building, where their attack had happened.

The building itself was now leveled to the ground. Calum frowned, not remembering the extent of the devastation. They had gone in silently, taking out the Iranian team with two other SEAL teams, mostly Terk's team only in a supervisory capacity. By the time it was all said and done, they were already on their way home. It had been smooth, efficient, successful—just the way they liked to do business.

At the same time, killing was hard for Cal to swallow, even if killing the bad guys was the right thing to do. He had known that, by killing that Iranian team, Terk's team had saved hundreds of their own people through this assigned mission.

Initially Cal thought that he might get used to it, but it never seemed to get any easier on him. He'd been looking forward to retiring, spending time just with his family, relaxing into some form of normalcy, ever since Terk's team was due to be disbanded. Who was he kidding? Cal thought of retirement since the formation of Terk's team. Now Calum had the chance to do that. And yet here he was again, … looking to save his family from whatever the hell this nightmare was that was chasing him and his team. And it was hard on him, always hard.

He kept moving in his mind's eye through the area, through time, but this part of Iran was dead. Nothing was there now, and, if anything had survived their attack, the remnants were long gone and had probably been intentionally moved. Nobody in their right mind would have stayed exactly in the same location where such devastation had been unleashed.

But then Cal frowned and reconsidered that because, in reality, some people would stay in the hope that they could manage their feelings and the emotional turmoil they were going through. Unable to walk away from the scene, they may be working on their need for … vengeance. Just no way to know for sure.

He needed to tell the team that the location was completely gone, but it was almost pointless to relay something they all seemed to know. The satellite imagery should have shown them that anyway. But then he frowned because, what if someone had access to that same satellite? Someone on the Iranian team might know where the US SEAL attackers had moved to afterward.

Calum didn't think his team was tracking the area, considering it safe now since they had supposedly removed their target. From what Calum saw—sensed—the area wasn't secure. Calum pulled back out, got up, and shook off the remnants of the trip, then stepped out into the hallway.

He moved down to the common area and walked in. Immediately everyone stopped talking and looked at him expectantly. With all of those gazes looking at him so intently, he shook his head. "Hey, it was just a test run." Then he looked over at Terk. "You know that entire building is gone, right?"

"I know." He nodded.

"So, yes, no signs of life, and the building has been demolished. Nothing is there physically, which I assume has been obvious on the satellite."

"It is," Terk agreed quietly. "What we didn't know was whether it was just a cover for something else."

Calum frowned at that, thought about what he'd seen and felt, then shook his head. "No. That doesn't mean some activity isn't close by—and I did get a hint of that energy—but you and I both know that I need an exact location in order to look into something like that remotely."

"Got it." Terk gave a gentle smile. "And that's good news. One less building to keep under surveillance."

"I get that," Calum agreed, "but it doesn't get us any further." He reached up and rubbed his head.

"How is the headache?"

"How do you know I have a headache?" he asked briskly.

"Well, the head rubbing is definitely indicative," he murmured, "but so is the crease on your forehead and the pain in your voice." Terk's voice was laced with concern for him.

Calum was annoyed with everything, and himself, for not being any help. "It's just—the trip wasn't that easy to do. Not anymore."

"No, it isn't. I get that. Using our abilities right now, with the chaos and all the hassles, is a pain in the ass. Everything is hurting, and that makes it much harder."

"Why is that, Terk? See? I get it, but I don't understand

it."

"Well, you've been injured for one thing," Terk replied.

At that, Damon piped up. "And it seems like none of us are operating at full capacity. We were, ... before all this," "but now everything seems like slogging through molasses."

Calum looked at him in surprise. "So it's happening to you too then?" His question was directed to team members present.

Damon nodded.

"Me too," Wade chimed in.

Cal looked around. "Gage too? Where is he?"

Terk nodded. "Gage's doing a perimeter check outside. And, yes, he's reporting the same side effects."

"Interesting. So how do we fix that?" Cal asked. "I don't really like being at half power."

"No, none of us do." Wade laughed.

"So how do we fix it, Terk?" Calum asked bluntly. "I don't want to keep operating like this."

Everyone looked over at Terk, who was all smiles. "You guys know how to power up and how to power down," he began, trying to calm them. "You don't need me for that."

"No, but this seems like it's a little past that," Calum stated cautiously.

"It really isn't," Terk replied. "This is definitely more about getting yourself back up and running. We've had pitfalls like this before—"

"Not like this," Calum protested vehemently.

The other two team members looked over at Terk. "Nothing like this," Damon confirmed.

Terk nodded. "Okay, so it's worse than anything we've gone through before. I get that, but the process is the same. You decide how much power you'll lose, and then you reclaim the rest of it."

"Are you saying that somebody else is affecting our ability to reclaim our power?"

"They have," he stated. "This whole scenario has affected your abilities. You've all become victims." Terk's tone remained calm and serene. "And that means you have to reclaim that part of you and get out of that mentality."

They stared at him in shock.

"Is that all it takes?" Calum asked in a hard tone.

"Yes. You are back up already and functioning again," he noted, "so I don't expect it will take you very long to make that mental switch."

Damon stared at him. "Mental switch? Are you saying this is in our heads? This is something that we're allowing to happen to us?"

"While you were injured? While you were in a coma? No. But, once you got your energy back," he explained, "and don't take this the wrong way, but, on a certain level, you handed over your power."

At that, Damon shook his head. "You know that I don't like hearing that shit."

"I know." Terk gave him a gentle smile. "You know how much I don't like seeing you guys go through this too, right?" They winced and murmured their acquiescence all around, acutely aware of the energy and effort Terk had invested in their recoveries.

They all shared a look.

Wade shrugged. "We've been through recovery exercises like that before," he admitted, "and you've made it very clear that it's something we can change."

"It is," Terk agreed. "You just need to make the decision to do so."

"*Great*," Cal muttered. "Of all the things we didn't think we would have to do today …"

At that, Terk laughed heartily. "You each need to decide to do whatever it is you think you ultimately need to do," he stated. "Give yourself full permission to do whatever you need to in order to regain that ability inside you. You all have something to protect. You all have something to defend. So ensure you're up to full power. Things happened in your lives, and that's damn bad, but now you need to be back up and running."

"It can't be that simple," Wade argued, walking closer. "We've all had our abilities damaged. In fact, you even said so yourself, Terk."

Immediately Terk nodded. "Absolutely, yet, in every step of the way, as each one of you gets stronger again, you're producing more and more of the same energy that each of you can utilize. But, so far, you're not doing that. You're not taking that team energy because you're afraid of hurting each other."

"Ah." Damon nodded. "Now that makes more sense. And that's why we're not back to full speed … because we're making sure our energy expenditures keep pace with the rest of the team."

Terk smiled and nodded. "You got it. And I love the protective sentiment. I really do. But, at this point, it's not helpful."

"No, it isn't," Calum confirmed. "How is Rick doing?"

"He's okay," Terk replied, "but he's lost in the ethers. I'm not exactly sure how to get him back again."

"What do you mean by lost? Like *lost*, lost, or can we get him back?" Gage asked in surprise.

"Well, for the moment, he'll stay there, but I really hope

it won't be for too long," Terk stated. "I might have to find somebody to pull him back out."

"Who would that be?" Calum asked.

At that, Terk gave him a lopsided grin. "You all have partners," he noted, "or at least all of you had partners you'd walked away from or kept at a distance."

"Jesus, Rick too?" Wade asked. The men stared at each other and then back at Terk. "That's one hell of a set of secrets that we've kept from each other."

"It absolutely is." Terk nodded. "And that's part of the reason it's so important for all of us to get this dealt with, so everybody can get back to having a life again."

"And then what?" Calum asked. "I had initially planned on retiring."

"And is that still how you feel?" Wade asked, turning to look at him. "We get that you've got a son. You're the only team member who has a child at the moment. But that also gives you more reason to help protect the world from some of these organizations."

"Exactly," Calum agreed, "so, yeah, I'm not sure about it yet."

"And you may not want to make that kind of decision without somebody else's input either." Wade gave Calum a lopsided grin.

"I think she has given up on trying to convince me to do something other than what I say I'll do."

"Sure, but she can be a huge support, or she can be a huge draw on your time—and energy," Damon noted. "Having somebody there supporting you is special. Some-body who understands who you are and why you're doing what you're doing is priceless."

Calum stared at him for a long moment. "No, you're

quite right, and Mariana is very patient."

"So you have something that's even more precious." Tasha stood up, then walked over to Damon, slipping her hand into his. "We both deliberately held off on developing any kind of relationship, thinking it would not be a good thing as coworkers. But we were wrong. I think it was important just to have that balance in our lives. To have something in our lives that makes us smile at the end of the day is awesome," she stated simply.

Calum looked at her beautiful grin, and, with a nod to Damon, Cal smiled. "Well, I'm glad you finally got him convinced that it's worthwhile. We all saw it, but he was a little bit on the slow side." He was clearly teasing them, and she was smiling, clearly happy.

"Sometimes he still is slow, but I'm working on it," she added gently.

Calum laughed at that. "Good, I'm really glad to hear it. I always knew you two were meant to be together."

"So did he. He was just being stubborn." She laughed.

"Hey, do you guys mind? I'm right here," Damon called out in protest.

"Yeah, you sure are." She gave him an eye roll. "Now, if only you weren't quite so stubborn about staying here."

At that, he kissed her hard, "*Ha-ha*, funny." Then he looked over to Terk.

"Considering your advice from earlier," Wade said, coming back to the main topic, "I'll go spend some *me time* to check your theory and to see if I can power up."

"You do that," Terk replied.

For the first time, Calum realized how exhausted Terk was. Cal frowned as he turned to Damon. "Has Terk been giving us all our energy, all this time?"

At that, Damon immediately nodded. "Yeah, that's why we need to take more responsibility."

"Jesus, I hadn't even considered what I was doing. It felt good, and I was doing better, so I just let it all ride. But, of course, it's a drain on him." Calum frowned, pivoting to face Terk.

"And it's a drain I'm happy to have," Terk stated immediately. "But energy needs to happen individually now, and it needs to happen fast."

"Yes, it does," Calum murmured, "and it will probably be faster than you expect it."

At that, Terk stared but didn't say any more.

Life was like that, and living with the team included a lot of things that were easy to deal with, and then there was all the rest. And none of it was easy at this point in time.

As Wade left, Damon looked over at Cal. "If you can recharge," he noted, "the best way to do it is with that family of yours."

Cal nodded. "In that case, I'll go see them." And he spun on his heels and left.

MARIANA WOKE FROM a deep sleep but with a sudden sense of impending doom. She wanted to rise from the bed, but a sweaty little boy weighed her down. She also couldn't figure out exactly what she was sensing. When the door opened, she gasped, only to recognize immediately that it was Cal.

"It's all right," he whispered. "I just came to get some rest."

She smiled. "Well, that's better than a lot of things I've heard recently," she murmured.

He walked over, studied the small double bed, then shifted the sleeping boy off to the side, and crawled in on the other side of her, facing his wife. "That's much better."

She chuckled, as he wrapped her in his arms. "Well, I'm certainly not against it," she murmured, "but it's not exactly the way I thought today would go."

"Nope," he replied. "I don't think any of us did. The question is, are you okay with it?"

"I'm okay with it, and I've been doing a lot of thinking."

"You, and all the rest of us too." He smiled.

"Any answers?" she asked.

"Not particularly. An awful lot is going on in our world that we can't sort out just yet. We have feelers out everywhere, and it will all come together, but it might take a few more days."

She felt a jolt of surprise at that. "Just days?"

"I would hope so," he said, "but I can't honestly swear to it."

"No, of course not," she murmured. "It would be nice to think it would get resolved that quickly."

"You're right. I suspect it'll be a lot longer than that." He shrugged. "But ... maybe not. It's really hard to know what's going on, but we obviously are under attack by somebody, and trying to keep everyone safe is the priority."

She agreed with that. "So, do we stay, or do we leave?" she asked bluntly. "Are we safer here with you or away from you?"

"For years, I've kept you away from me to keep you safe," he admitted, "and you were still taken anyway."

She smiled, but he looked distraught, like the darkness had an arm around his neck. "In that case, I hope we stay with you. Yet it's not a life for our son."

He hesitated, then nodded. "Yes, but what if it's longer?"

"Well, Little Calum would rather spend time with his father than be locked away somewhere, where we don't have any kind of a life," she murmured. "And I can see that being your next option because, given a choice, you just want to keep us safe, where nobody can get near us."

He laughed. "That would be a choice, ... but obviously not a good one. I know that that's not something this little guy would like, nor is it healthy for him."

"Nope, it absolutely is not," she agreed cheerfully. "That doesn't mean that I still don't know you though."

He smiled. "What I don't understand is how I ever thought I could live without you."

"Did you tell them all about me?"

"Terk already knew, and the others found out when they rescued you," he shared. "But they knew the decision I made wasn't made lightly. Whether they agreed with it or not, I don't know. Obviously something has changed within the team dynamic too." And then he explained about the other relationships.

"Interesting," she noted. "I love it, as a romantic, thinking that love conquers all. But I'm also a realist, and, after being kidnapped and our son put in danger, I'm not sure I can believe that kind of stuff anymore."

"Of course not. It's about real-life loving and making sure that you still are as safe as can be."

"Agreed," she murmured. "So where is that point with us?"

"I'm not sure yet. I mean, if you want, I can send you home, hire some security, or maybe send you to your family."

"But then if anything happens—"

"Right. If anything happens, we're even farther away. No civilian will know what to do, and it could be an even worse scenario." He was talking to himself, rambling mostly, trying to reach a decision. "Maybe, or it could be a much better one. Yet we can't assume it'll be a worse one."

"I don't know. I tend to feel really pessimistic when it comes to this stuff. I didn't enter into a relationship with you lightly, but having a child has changed some things. I need to keep him safe," she stated. "I'm no longer as convinced as you that being apart is safer."

"Well, that's because you were just kidnapped." He rubbed his nose against her cheek. "Something I would have done anything to have stopped. I'm so sorry."

"And I know that," she told him gently. "I don't hold you responsible."

"You should. Almost anybody else would."

"So, it's decided then." She smiled. "We're staying with you because it's safer and because, if time is short, I don't want to lose any more of it." He hesitated, and she shook her head vehemently. "No. Enough. We tried it your way, and we were still taken. So now we'll try it my way, and hopefully it will go much better."

"And if it doesn't?"

She looked at him. "The one thing that you have to understand is that this is about trust. And I trust that you will keep us safe." He winced at that. "Does it seem like I'm being unfair?" she asked.

"No," he replied instantly, "but it won't help me to sleep better at night."

"But how could you possibly sleep at night anyway?" she asked. "At least when we're here and under your wing, we all know that we're safe," she explained in a reasonable tone of voice. "And when you're away? Well, it is what it is."

He pulled her close and just held her.

"I'm not leaving, at least not now, so don't even mention it."

He groaned. "How did you know I was trying to figure out how to say that?"

"Because I know you. We've been together a long time."

"We have. … It hurt me a lot to send you away."

"And I get that," she noted, "but I'm done with being sent away. It wasn't just you who was hurt by that. You hurt me too. I thought you didn't care." When he snorted at that, she smiled against his neck. "And, therefore, this way, everything is fine. This living situation may or may not continue—and your work after this may or may not continue."

He was startled by her announcement.

"Do you think I'm a fool? I certainly recognize that you're doing important work, and I understand that, at some point in time, you'll be ready to walk away, but I'm not sure that time is now. And, if other couples can make it work, why can't we make it work as well?"

"But are they making it work?" he asked in an almost desperate tone of voice. "If things go wrong, the repercussions are terrible."

"They are," she agreed quietly. "I get that, and I know you will do your utmost to look after that. But, if things go wrong for you, it'll be bad for us, no matter where we are."

"I understand that Ice and Levi have started a family," he stated, "but that's different."

She looked at him, her gaze flat.

"Well, maybe it's different. I don't know anymore," he murmured. "It seemed like it was different."

"But see? I don't think it is," she argued. "I don't think it's different at all. I think it's all about doing the best you can and realizing that evil people like these after the team will always be out there in the world and that you are part of the team who hunts them down," she explained. "Can you choose not do that anymore? Maybe, but, if it would crush you to walk away before you are truly ready, that's not a good answer either. And that's just a completely different aspect that we must look at."

"What about you?" he asked in a challenging tone of voice. "Don't you want to have a career or something else in your life?"

"Maybe at some point in time," she replied, "but right now? No. ... Motherhood is my career. I know for a lot of women that doesn't work, and others would laugh at me, but I don't care. You need to do what you need to do. I will do what is needed to be done to keep Little Calum safe."

She wasn't making a big deal of it all, and she had her priorities straight. She also knew that she would take some flak from other people, who thought motherhood alone didn't define her enough or that she was living through her child or not even attempting to support herself. She wasn't too bothered by what other people said, as long as she got to stay with her husband and carve out some kind of a family life. "There has to be some way," she whispered, "for us to have more family time than this."

"I haven't talked to the others about it yet," he began, "but I would think that everybody is looking for more of it as well."

"So that's good, and whatever you guys do to rebuild needs to take that into account. And whatever you do decide," she stated in a firm voice, "I'll be here."

He smiled. "You might change your mind," he noted, "when Little Calum gets older."

She looked up at her husband, amused, a twinkling set of mischief in her eyes. "You might too. And, sure, we might have to change location, and we might have to do all kinds of things. Maybe we'll set up something similar to the compound Levi and Ice have," she added. "Do you really think all the couples in your team out there won't have children themselves at some point in time?"

He frowned, as he thought about it. "I know that is something Tasha has always wanted."

"And Tasha will get it," Mariana stated softly. "These are natural instincts for a lot of women. It's something that's really important, and not everybody is willing to walk away without them."

"But, given the danger, it seems crazy," he muttered.

"I get it, but there must be a way to handle this … balance, and the more of these bad guys you get rid of now," she suggested, "the less we have to worry about down the road."

He chuckled. "The only problem with that thinking is …" And he looked down at her, with a sly grin.

"I know. More bad guys are always coming out of the woodwork. I get it. So let's just table this discussion for a moment," she said firmly. "Rest. You need it." When he opened his mouth, she placed a finger against his lips. "No arguments, cowboy. Time for a snooze. Let's just drift off into a peaceful empty space, where you can rest and re-charge."

Her use of the word *recharge* was a bit on the nose, and he almost laughed at how she had chosen it.

"You need to let it go for now," she added. "I know perfectly well a lot is going on in your world."

"Funny, when did you become so bossy?"

"I didn't spend all these years with you and not realize you have some abilities you don't talk about." He looked at her in surprise, and she shrugged. "And, no, we're not talking about it now. Just know that I know, and it's fine. I guessed quite a bit, and Tasha had some answers for me. Right now, you need to recharge and to rest. You've been hurt, and you're pretty well whacked out from whatever happened to you and to your team," she admitted. "You can't help any of us if you're not up to snuff yourself." Her tone spoke volumes. "Now, close your eyes. I'll stay here while you sleep."

Calum knew it was futile to argue, so he settled in and almost instantly drifted off to sleep.

She smiled, as she looked over at their son. She meant what she had said. She had fought long and hard to get to this point, and she wouldn't be stashed away again, like last time. *Somewhere safe and out of sight* hadn't in itself kept them safe. They were a family, and she wanted to live like one. Knowing everything now, she could then do what was she needed to do to keep them safe, and she wasn't planning on her and their child being sent away again.

CHAPTER 2

W HEN MARIANA WOKE up, she was surprised to find
Little Calum still sleeping, tucked up beside her in the
bed. Cal was gone. That man moved like a ghost, and
sometimes she wondered if he wasn't one. She could hear
him—and many times sense him—in ways that she knew no
normal person could.

She toyed with the idea of it just being the closeness that
they shared, but more recently she had realized it was
something completely different. Something that nobody
could really explain. She'd almost given up on Cal. They had
been separated for so long, and she wasn't sure if that even
mattered to him. Once their son started struggling to
remember that his dad even existed, Mariana knew she was
in trouble.

Instead she decided to talk to her husband and to figure
out what was going on. They had hoped to reconcile after he
retired, but, when all hell blew up, with the dismantling of
his team and the attack on them shortly thereafter, she
figured she'd lost him. At that point in time everything
became crystal clear. She would do whatever she could to
keep Cal close, to keep him safe, and to avoid getting caught
up in that mindset of losing versus *not* losing.

She had never doubted that he was trying to keep her
safe—but at what cost? She understood the price now, and

she was no longer willing to pay it. She understood that so much was going on that she couldn't begin to fathom, but she had to make him realize that, even if they only had a little bit of time left together, it was still worth it. Being together was the key.

He would do everything he could to keep them safe, she was certain of that. And maybe he would even be more careful himself, knowing they were here and waiting. She didn't know for sure, and she didn't think he took unnecessary risks anyway, but, when he had contacted her out of the blue, with the news that the group was being disbanded and that he wanted to talk to her, she'd been overjoyed. She had planned on not giving him a chance to talk at all, just pulling him back into her world and keeping him there.

It didn't work out that way. He had been badly injured instead. They all had been badly injured.

She hated even the reminder of all the nightmare scenarios she'd thought of during the time that he'd been under. Terk had done everything he could to keep her informed, all she wanted was to be there at Calum's side while somehow protecting Little Calum from this harsh reality as well.

She hadn't wanted to subject her son to sitting at his father's bedside for hours, on and on till the end, not knowing if Cal would even wake up. She wondered whether Cal would have come to her, when he woke up after all this, or would use it as yet another excuse to avoid her.

Maybe she owed the kidnappers a *thank you* for that. Because, now that she was here, she was in a better place. She and Cal and Little Calum were all in a better place, and no way in hell was she leaving without giving it a second chance. It seemed odd to think along those lines, but one had to do what one had to do.

She thought back to the kidnapping, remembering how terrified Little Calum had been and how she'd worked to keep him calm. Thankfully the kidnappers hadn't been physically cruel as much as mentally cruel. She hadn't thought hurting her and her son had been in the plan, just that they were the means to an end. And, as such, she wondered if something she might have heard would make more sense now.

As she lay here quietly, she focused, only remembering that discussion about Sean and how Calum would hate it and how Sean had been waiting for it a long time. At least she had remembered that and had told Terk and Cal, but surely she could remember more, wishing she had asked a few more questions of her kidnappers.

Just then Little Calum woke up, staring at her groggily, with sleepy eyes. "I'm hungry."

She winced at that. "Well, that's a good sign. I will go find us some food."

"No." His arms clutched her tighter. He was frightened.

"Ah," she murmured, "well, how about we get Daddy to bring you some food?"

Immediately he raised his head, his eyes wide. "Daddy here?"

She smiled and whispered, "Yes, sweetie. Daddy is here."

He immediately pushed himself upright and looked around.

"Let me call him." She grabbed her phone and sent him a text, since she didn't know what Calum was doing. It wasn't but moments later when the door opened, and Cal stepped inside. Little Calum took one look at his daddy and burst into tears, holding out his arms.

Calum took several strong strides toward him, grabbed

him up in his arms, and held him tight. "It's okay, buddy. You're okay. Everything is okay."

But Little Calum wasn't to be appeased. He wouldn't let go of his father's arms. She gave Cal a look, affirming how much he was needed. Cal just nodded and held the little boy close. The sheen of tears in her husband's eyes brought on the tears in her own.

Why the hell he ever thought leaving us behind was a good idea is beyond me. She knew she had to put those thoughts out of her head for now and to backtrack very quickly. She needed to be in the present. "Any chance of a shower?"

He nodded. "Absolutely, and we need to get some food for you guys."

At that, Little Calum pulled his head back and smiled up at his father eagerly. "Food, Daddy, food."

"I got this." He nodded. "Mommy can have a shower, and we can surely work something out."

"On our own?" Little Calum asked, clearly excited. Part of him wanted to scramble down, out of his father's arms, but the other part wouldn't let him. He didn't want to, not just yet.

Mariana let them be and escaped to the bathroom. There, she stood for a moment, her arms wrapped around her chest. She had to find a way to make this work; she had to. Ensuring that her child felt safe was important to her. Beyond important. They couldn't keep going as they had been; that had led them straight to the exit door of splitting for good. But now? Now she felt like they had been given a second chance.

She hopped into the shower, where nobody could hear her softly sobbing, and she let the tears roll. By the time she stepped out, she figured she'd wasted enough time and quickly got dressed in the same clothes she had been kidnapped in. They would need clothes and other belongings too. When she stepped out of the bathroom, she looked over at Cal, and the sight of him holding Little Calum turned up the heat on all her emotions. The two of them looked up and smiled, so delighted with each other.

"We need to get some clothes for him too," she noted, "and a few other things, toiletries, maybe some vitamins."

"That's fine," Calum replied. "We can arrange all that."

She nodded and looked over at her son. "I thought you and Daddy would already be looking for food."

"He said we had to wait for you." Little Calum rubbed his eyes. She dressed quickly.

"Dear God, why did I ever think we needed to separate?" Calum asked, his voice a bit off, as he watched her.

She gave him a hard stare, as she stepped into her shoes. "I don't know, but I was thinking the same thing in the bathroom just now. You better not be considering a repeat."

With emotions choking him, Calum just shook his head but didn't say any more.

"Let's go find some food," she added.

Cal nodded, and, swinging his son in his arms, he led the way out the bedroom door.

Mariana walked down the hall and into the main common area to hear a sudden silence all around them. She smiled nervously. "So I am Mariana, Cal's secret. The one I'm guessing everyone knows about."

The others chuckled, as Tasha immediately walked over and held out her hand. "Not really, we're all kind of in the same boat these days. I'm Tasha." Her tone was kind. "Now, to set the record straight, some of use knew that he had been married at some point in the past but didn't know that he had a family now."

"Yeah," Mariana replied, "I was really hoping it wouldn't end up breaking completely off for good, but it was looming large and looking inevitable, before all this trouble started."

"Well, hopefully now that you've been reunited, you can work it out," Tasha stated firmly. Looking at Little Calum, she reached over and gently touched his cheek. "Who is this adorable little guy?" she asked.

"That little fella is Calum Jr.," Mariana replied, amusement in her voice.

"That'll get a little confusing." Damon chuckled, as he walked over. "Hey, big guy. You got the same name as your daddy, *huh*?"

Little Calum nodded but stayed quiet and content in Calum's strong arms. Mariana watched the interaction, knowing it would take him a bit of time. Not too long, as he was incredibly outgoing, but it would take a bit to get comfortable with all these strangers, especially due to the kidnapping. "We generally call him Little Calum."

"Food!" Little Calum cried out joyously, as he spotted the table. She laughed, and they walked over to have a look. Mariana smiled as she watched her son studying the contents of the table with interest.

"We may not have a whole lot of kid-friendly food here," Damon noted.

"We can do toast," Tasha suggested immediately. "We don't have any cereal though."

"Toast would be fine," Mariana replied. "Do you have any peanut butter?"

"Oh, yeah, Wade practically lives on it." Tasha looked toward Sophia. "We've got plenty."

So, with Tasha's help, they quickly got a meal going.

Mariana knew that once Little Calum started looking for food, he got hungry very quickly, and his temper didn't allow for much patience in the matter. He would need food and fast. And, sure enough, by the time the toast was ready, he was starting to whine.

In a way, food was the weakness of this clan. Cal and Little Calum both got grumpy about food. As soon as Mariana got some toast in her son's mouth, he shut up and just kept eating. The others laughed. Wade walked over, smiled at Little Calum, and joked about the peanut butter. He was uncertain if the little guy recognized him or if he could even sort out the rescuers from the kidnappers in his memory.

"You know what? ... We really have to change our living arrangements," Wade noted quietly.

"I get that this is no place for a kid." She nodded. "But, if you're thinking about stuffing us away in some safe house," she began, her gaze laser focused, openly glaring at them, "alone, ... you better think again." She made absolutely no apologies for the hard edge in her voice.

Wade stared at her in surprise and then gave her a nod. "Got it. I see you're in the same boat as the rest of the women."

"Well, I doubt that any of us would appreciate being summarily lumped together with such limited knowledge, but, if what you mean is that we share the same position of wanting to stay close, then, yes, you are correct," Mariana confirmed. "I would never presume to speak for the others, but I definitely will speak for myself. We've done without Cal for a long time, with only occasional random visits, and that will stop now."

Calum opened his mouth and then frowned and didn't

say anything, as she nodded.

"Good choice," she stated, "and it's a really good time to just be quiet. We've agreed that, despite the best of intentions, we've got to do better by our son."

"Which is precisely why we need a solution," said Terk. Coming up beside her, he reached down, gave her a hug. "It's good to see you," he murmured.

"Did I ever say *thank you* for that rescue?" She gave him a wry smile.

"No thanks needed," he replied. "We're sorry you wound up in that scenario in the first place."

"Did you catch them all?"

"We got most of them," he replied, "and now we need Cal here to put us in touch with the Iranian group."

She shrugged. "I assume that means a lot to you or to the larger effort, so that's good, but, for me, I just want to know if those assholes who kidnapped us are gone."

"They are," Cal stated, "and now I'm going after Sean. And the question is what to do with you while I'm away on a hunt."

"Well, for the moment," she suggested, "we can just stay here. As long as the food holds out, I'll have no problem keeping our son here and happy." Calum hesitated, and she waved a hand in the air. "Go. Don't waste your time arguing. The sooner we get this dealt with, the better."

With a bark of laughter, Terk said, "Isn't that the truth."

Calum frowned and looked over at the others, perhaps hoping for backup.

Tasha immediately shook her head. "None of that, Cal. You got to do what you got to do, ... and we'll be right here, doing what we got to do."

"And that includes keeping an eye on us, I suppose?"

Mariana wondered if she should be offended. Yet, at the same time, the relief on Cal's face was evident.

"Look, Cal," Tasha told him. "Times have changed. We've all been through a lot, and there is no going back, no more of this keeping our private lives separate from our work lives. We have changed, and our lives will be different. After this, several relationships will finally get the attention they deserve. Relationships that probably shouldn't have been put on hold in the first place," she snorted. "If we've learned nothing else, it should be that life is too short and too unpredictable to spend it apart from those we are meant to be with. None of us are looking to break up over this. In the meantime, you two have family here, and we will all do our best to protect it."

The sincerity in Tasha's words came through, and Mariana felt the truth behind them. She needed to make this work. "I'm sorry if my words sounded rude and unappreciative, Tasha. I'm just overreacting. Cal, you go do your thing. Just make sure you come back."

He smiled gently at her. "Will do." He walked over, and he kissed her hard. "Hold that thought until I get back," he growled into her ear.

She smiled as she watched him kiss Little Calum, happily eating, before Cal walked to the rear door. It was so hard to watch him leave, when he had only just returned to her life, and she was desperate to hold back the tears. The moment he went through the back door, she sagged into the closest kitchen chair. She knew the other women were watching her, and it was all she could do to keep from falling into the whirlwind of worry and despair again.

When a cup of coffee promptly landed in front of her, her smile lit the room. "Now *that* I could really use." She looked up at Terk, smiled, and her tone was affectionate. "You always did know what I was thinking."

He shrugged.

"Well, didn't you?"

"Part of my charm," he teased, with hint of a smile.

"Well, I don't know about charm," she noted, "but definitely part of the scary aspect of your personality."

He looked at her, completely serious. "Scary, *huh?* Really?"

"No, not so much. Not now," she murmured. "I've gotten used to it. The same way I've gotten used to a lot of things that I never thought I would. Yet we could never convince Cal that this is where I needed to be."

"Well, having you here now is likely to affect that too," Terk pointed out.

She nodded. "I hope you also don't think that I should be disappearing because this boy needs his father."

"But we also need everybody to stay safe, so that gives us a challenge."

"You're up for it." She waved a hand in a dismissive way. "You'll fix it."

He laughed. "Glad you're so convinced. Things are a bit of a mess right now."

"In many ways." She gave him a flat look. "I never expected us to get kidnapped, but, now that it's happened, I'm almost ready to thank them."

He stared at her in surprise, until he realized what she meant, and slowly nodded. "It'll take a lot to convince Cal," Terk noted. "This will seem awfully idyllic, but it's not reality."

"Of course it's not reality," she murmured. "Reality would be easier."

"You could be right. The fact of the matter is, it's never that easy."

"No, it's not," she agreed, "and I don't need our lives to be easy, but I do plan to make sure that, whatever happens next, we're with him."

"I'll do my best, Mariana, to make that happen," Terk replied quietly. "I'll do my best."

She knew that he meant it. They had communicated in some ways that she didn't understand, and, because of that, she also knew who he was on the inside. His best was pretty damn good, and he didn't say things that he didn't mean.

"YOU OKAY, CAL?" Wade asked, as he and Damon and Cal slipped through the alleyway beyond the warehouses where their temporary headquarters were. Terk had vehicles stashed nearby, and they were taking the long way to one of them, watching for tails or street cams or drones or anything suspicious.

"I'm fine." Calum shrugged. "It's just weird."

"Yeah, you're not kidding. We're all kind of in the same boat," Wade admitted.

"After months, years really," Damon shared, "of keeping ourselves separate and away for the safety of others, ... now here we are—in a position where we won't really have any say in the matter anymore."

They were all awestruck, and really in shock. Emotions were their kryptonite.

Hearing Damon say it out loud, Calum gave a shout of laughter. "Yeah, you guys got that impression from her too, *huh?*"

"Unless you're dead set against having her back in your life," Wade noted, "I'll say you're done."

"That's the impression I've come to as well."

"Unless of course you don't want to." Damon looked over at him.

"What? No. ... All I ever wanted was to have my family close."

"And yet you still came on board. Why?"

"Because my family was killed in a terrorist bomb attack," he stated, "and I felt like I needed to do something with the world to help rid it of more of the same."

"That's understandable too," Damon murmured.

"But it also means that I know just what the hell is going on out there, and I don't want to take any chances." Calum held his body rigid, his hand fisted, protective style.

Damon may not know every detail in Cal's life, but he understood Cal, as did the others. They'd been a team for a long time. "We have to find a way to make this work."

"And then we'll just retire after this?" Calum asked, shaking his head.

"I can't see that happening any time soon," Wade replied.

"And yet it needs to, if we all have families, kids, doesn't it?" Damon frowned, as he looked over at the others.

"According to Mariana, we're supposed to set up something like Levi has," Calum shared, "where we can have a family life and hire other people to do this kind of work."

"Can we though?" Wade asked drily. "Just think about it. You know what kind of work we do. Energy work is not exactly anything we can toss off on other people. But maybe we can do it in a more distant way somehow."

"That's sounds absurd," Damon pitched in.

But now Calum rambled on and on. "What if nobody even knows that it's us? What if we do a massive name change. Buy a compound someplace where we can defend ourselves, if need be. We can keep everyone safe, and we have to just keep everybody close," he murmured.

"I don't know, Cal." Damon paused. "Maybe I just … I don't know. So much is going on right now that nobody can say what our future will be."

"Exactly." Calum agreed. "That's why we need to just keep going and doing what we have to do, and then we'll figure it out."

"If only it were that easy." Damon shook his head.

"I'm hoping it's that easy," Cal replied. "I'm hoping that some answers are out there for us because we need them. There's got to be something that we can do to make things a whole lot safer for the world and for ourselves."

"We *were* doing it, Calum"—Damon was on the verge of a rage—"until somebody decided that we were more dangerous than the enemy and that we needed to be taken down a notch or two. That's the thing that really hurts," Damon stated, trying to keep his emotions in check. "To think that our own government did this? … After all the work we've done and all we've given up? It just makes me so damn mad."

"We don't know that for sure," Wade noted.

"No, we don't, but it sure is suspicious," Damon stated.

"Okay, so where are we going then?" Calum asked.

"To check on an address registered to Sean Calvert's father."

Calum looked at him, startled. "Wow. How come I didn't get any intel on that?"

"Because we were doing the briefing while you were recharging with your family."

"Ah, shit. Okay, so you want to bring me up to date then?"

Damon and Wade quickly told Cal what they had unearthed about this Sean Calvert guy from the Netherlands, having relocated to Belgium, then to England where his father had property.

"Interesting," Cal said. "Anybody question why England was a location for these guys?"

"Probably the tax laws or something," Damon replied, sounding a bit coy. "We also knew of quite a hub of terrorist activity in England for a while, and they're getting harder and harder to ferret out and track. They are spreading like the Hydra heads—cut one off, and two spring back. We take one out, only to find a bunch of others."

"I know, right?" Cal nodded. "We've sure seen that happen a few times. And in pretty short order."

"Yeah," Wade added, "but these terrorists are tenacious. We finally get the head of one group cut off and get them down for a while, and then they pop back up, just as ugly again."

"So this address, it looks like an empty property?" Damon guessed.

"I can check out the address beforehand and see," Calum stated.

"Can you do it on the fly?" Damon asked.

"Well, not nearly as well as I used to travel on the ethers, but I am getting things back stronger and stronger."

"Welcome to the club, though we're all making progress it seems," Wade noted.

"Terk also mentioned that being with your family would do that faster for you than anything." Damon cocked an eyebrow to Cal.

"Turns out he's right about that, as much as I hate to admit it," Cal confirmed. "She grounds me in a way I hadn't really noticed before, but now that I need that grounding, it's really obvious." He hesitated for a moment, then went on tentatively. "She also said something in passing about the way Terk has been communicating with her."

At that, Wade and Damon both froze.

"Do you think she can communicate telepathically with him?" Damon asked Cal.

"I don't know. I haven't had a chance to really sit down and talk to her about it," Cal replied, "but it wouldn't surprise me."

"Interesting," Wade murmured. "You know what? I guess it would make sense that we're each collecting women who understand the challenges we have with our special skills alone, as well as the risky work we do."

"And potentially have some of their own needs or challenges at the same time," Damon added.

"Well, it would be good if we did," Cal murmured, "if you think about it. ... Any more action at the government level?"

"No, though we have Lorelei here now, who is still working for them. They think she's at a hotel," Damon shared. "She just changed hotels again, saying she was trying to find one at a better price. They've asked her what her long-term plans are, and she says at the moment she doesn't have any. Of course she's working here, trying to track the allegiances in the US black ops areas, seeing who with connections is currently for or against us."

"Can she find out any of that?"

"We're hoping so," Wade murmured. "She is definitely

trying."

"We can't ask any more than that," Cal stated, "because this is one hell of a mess."

"It is, but we're getting somewhere, so hold on to that thought, and we'll be fine." Damon slapped him on the shoulder, as they all climbed into one of Terk's vehicles.

Cal smiled at their optimism. Just then he settled back into the seat, eyes closed for a moment. "The house is not vacant, by the way."

"I was just getting a heat signature off it myself," Damon confirmed. "I'm not very good at what you do, and, of course, I've been spreading my energy trying to protect the base and take some of the pressure off Terk."

"And you need to keep doing that too," both of the other men told him in unison.

"Don't worry. I'm not risking anybody's life by doing this," Damon murmured. "I'm just trying to operate at some level in a way that will give us more options."

"Well, I'm driving," Wade stated. "So you keep an eye out for signatures."

"Working on it," Damon murmured. "So far I'm not seeing anything recognizable."

"It doesn't mean you won't," Wade warned.

"Nope, it doesn't mean I won't."

As soon as they were only a few blocks away from Sean's house, Wade slowed down. "I'll do one pass."

"Good," Cal murmured. "I am definitely reading people are there."

"More than one heat signature?"

"I'll go in," Calum stated decisively, watching for any opposition from his team. The others shared a look but nodded, letting him travel the ethers. And he knew that was

just a sign of where things were at right now. They had to
work solo at times; there were no other options. They didn't
have enough people to keep all this going. And the team
members who were now conscious and on their feet? Well,
they were all working at around half capacity.

With a sigh, Cal closed his eyes and let his energy drift
toward the house, seeking the heat signatures. As he pushed
forward, he sensed more and more inside.

"There might be just one," he offered, after a moment.
Frowning, he shook his head. "I'll revise that. There is one,
but I don't think he's alive. His signature is too cool."

"Shit," Damon replied. "Do you know how many buildings we've been into the last few days? How many people we
found? Nothing but dead bodies." He groaned.

"You sure a live one is still in there?" Wade asked Cal.

"I can take another look, but it's kind of difficult ..."
And he stopped. "You know what? ... Give me a sec."
Calum was sweating like crazy in just seconds, probably due
to moving too fast on the psychic plane. "There might be
one who is alive, but he's not moving. It's like he's right
beside the dead body." At that, they looked at each other.
"He is at the dead body. They're both together, but I'm not
sure what he's doing."

"He could be searching it for something."

"He could be doing all kinds of stuff. We just don't have
enough information to know."

With that, Wade parked and they all got out of the vehicle.

As soon as they stopped to check their surroundings cautiously, Cal said, "I need to go in again, now that we are
closer."

"Are you sure about that, Cal?" Damon asked. "Don't

use up all your energy too soon."

Cal stopped, looked at his partners. "We never used to hesitate like this before."

"Yeah, it's a new thing," Damon replied. "It comes with being hunted and attacked, having our team taken down."

Calum looked far ahead, using his extra senses. "We were always safe before," he reminded them.

They nodded. "It was just a question, Cal," Damon replied. "Don't make it more than that."

"Right, okay. So, yes, I'm sure. One live body right at the dead one," and they exchanged a glance, as Calum took a step.

"So what is your plan?" Damon asked Cal.

"I'll meet you in"—he looked at his watch—"say, twenty minutes."

"And you're going into the main house?" Wade asked, for confirmation.

Cal nodded. "Not this way. An entrance is around back, so I'm heading there." And, with that, he took off.

CHAPTER 3

M ARIANA WAITED AS long as she could, and then, when there was nothing more for her to do, she got up and walked over to Terk. She needed something to keep herself busy, but, for now, she needed to keep Little Calum engaged. "Is there any chance of a laptop or TV or something Little Calum could watch?"

Terk looked at her and then nodded. "Yep, and paper and pens and coloring books. I collected all that kid-friendly stuff too," he noted, "and you can make me a list of what else you want."

She sat down with Little Calum and together they wrote a list of things that they wanted. She looked over at Terk. "Can we go back to the apartment I rented and get anything?"

"Absolutely not," he said. "You need to stay put. We'll reconsider that option in a day or two, as we free up some manpower. It might be Merk who does that."

She frowned, nodded. "Merk is here?" she asked.

Terk asked, "Do you know him?"

"Yes." She smiled. "Not as well as I would like to obviously, but I have had some exposure."

"*Exposure*, huh?"

She shrugged. "Yeah, that's one of the things that I need to talk to Cal about, and I just haven't had a chance."

"Meaning?"

She lowered her voice. "Meaning that, some of the things Cal does, I think I was—" She stopped.

"Go on."

"I think I was being linked in somehow." Terk slowly sat back and stared at her. Terk was confused now, and she shrugged. "I don't know how to explain that."

"Well, I suggest you try a little bit more because that was a very strange comment."

She winced. "I know, and he probably wouldn't appreciate it, but I haven't had a chance to discuss it with him. I thought you knew. At first, it was nothing. I thought maybe I was just imagining things. Then, out of the blue, I would hear more of his voice. Then it was a lot. Now it just seems like I'm much more connected to Cal than I ever thought I was."

"And is that good or bad? How do you feel about it? What is your sense of it?" Terk asked, looking at her seriously.

She stared at him. "How do I answer that? You always talk in circles."

"Not always."

"Yes, always. … It's like you only let us have half the information."

"Well, Mariana, that's because I usually only have half the information," he replied calmly.

"Is it really that bad?"

He nodded. "Yeah, it's really that bad. Sometimes I get a little bit more, and sometimes I don't."

She raised both hands, exasperated. "How can you operate successfully then?"

"Sometimes we don't," he admitted. "Sometimes it's a

regular shit storm."

She winced. "Like the attack on the team?"

"Yes," he agreed. "But, in all fairness, the team had been disbanded. We were just about done and were saying goodbye, when everything blew up."

"And what exactly was it that blew up?"

"It was like a percussion bomb in all our heads," he described. "Everybody was joking and having fun, and, the next thing I knew, they were all collapsed."

"And yet you weren't as badly affected."

He shook his head. "No, I wasn't."

There was something more to that story, but she knew Terk wasn't quite ready to tell her. "Fine, and ever since, … ever since Cal became conscious again, it's like I can read his thoughts. And I know that would not make him happy."

Terk stared at her in surprise. "Can you read anybody else's thoughts?" Terk's gaze narrowed on her.

"A connection of sorts—like when you told me things about Merk. Do you mean *really* read your thoughts? Then no. You're impossible anyway." At that, Tasha snorted, and Mariana realized they had everybody's attention. She looked over at them and frowned. "Sorry, I figured that if Cal knew, it would make our relationship easier, but I don't know that it makes it any easier at all."

"Believe me. Almost everybody here has some weird gift going on," Tasha confirmed. "Turns out you're not all that unusual." She shrugged. "Let's just say that Damon and I are getting closer than I ever thought was possible."

"Same here with me and Gage," Lorelei agreed, from the table off to the side.

At that, Sophia nodded. "I've wondered if it's a side effect of Wade's injuries or something." She looked from one woman to the other.

Terk took in all the women with one frowning sweep. "Let me get this straight. All four of you have now got some new connection to the men in your lives?" As one, they all nodded. "Wow." Terk stared at them each. "I didn't see that coming at all. I'll need more details on all this, in order to figure out just what's going on."

"Does it matter?" Tasha asked quietly. "The fact is, we are much more connected to our guys but also to the other men on this team. Yes, that definitely changes the dynamic."

"It absolutely does change the dynamic," Terk agreed. "The how and why of it though? I can't tell you at this point, and it's too early to have any idea if it's good, bad, or ugly. Because it's already happened, it doesn't really matter. But at least you are developing some deeper connections with your partners."

They all laughed at what was a long speech for this quiet, quirky man they all had come to adore.

"Well, that was my attitude. It's already there, so no need to fuss about it." Tasha was taking it pretty lightly, and she looked over at Mariana. "Does it bother you?"

"Bother me? No. It's …" She frowned for a moment. "You know what? Honestly it's kind of nice. It makes me feel closer to him. It makes me feel like I haven't been cast out in the world on my own."

The others winced.

"Yeah, I don't think I'd take that kindly either," Lorelei murmured.

"Yes, but it's not so different to your situation, is it?"

"No, well, yes. … I don't know. I really don't know. I mean, obviously in our cases, all of our cases, the men chose our safety over theirs."

Terk immediately shook his head. "No, you can't just put it down to that. It's about the safety of the entire team because, if one of us is compromised, then all of us are compromised. The fact of the matter is, if you're reading their thoughts and have some kind of a connection," Terk explained, "whenever they're compromised, you are now as well."

"That would go along well with the way I'm feeling," Tasha admitted.

"I'll give this some consideration," Terk replied thoughtfully.

"Not too much," Lorelei said cheerfully, "because I, for one, don't mind it. I like being connected on this level with Gage."

"I get it," Terk noted. "I've just never heard of it before."

At that, Tasha laughed. "But, then again, all of this is so new. And so much of what we have learned over time was never heard of before either."

He smiled at her. "I agree, but you might not want to tell them all at once."

Lorelei looked at Terk in surprise, then nodded. Tasha knew them well, as did Sophia by now.

"The team will adapt just fine in the end," Terk added. "As a matter of fact, this could probably make things easier on them in many ways. But it'll still be a bit of a shock."

Lorelei laughed. "I can hold off for a bit." Tasha and Sophia were on the same page, then Lorelei looked over at Mariana. "And what about you?"

"It would be hard not to tell him," she admitted slowly. "I can hold off too for a little bit, but I do feel like it's part of the larger conversations that Cal and I need to have."

"That's understandable, especially since your family has

only just been reunited," Lorelei noted. "How about if you have that conversation with Calum, and, once you do, you can tell us how it went? Then we'll all figure out how we'll handle it going forward."

With that, Mariana laughed. "So I get to be the guinea pig," she teased.

The other women immediately nodded, with smiles all around. "Absolutely."

Terk started to laugh. "I don't think it's a problem in any way. Honestly, I think the men will be delighted, but it's something they haven't considered. I can tell you that we have all discussed the possibility, so I don't think they'll be upset."

"Yeah, but thinking they won't be upset and having them actually not be upset are two very different things," Mariana noted. "I already feel like I'm only here because the kidnapping blew up in my face, so I don't really want to do anything to rock the boat. At the same time, I'm really not prepared to walk away and to divide our family anymore."

"You shouldn't have to," Tasha stated immediately.

Mariana smiled at her. "Thank you for that."

Terk just rolled his eyes. "Okay, ladies. I get that this is a bonding moment, but let's not forget the men are out there on a mission."

At that, everybody returned to their work.

"We've got one heat signature in the building," Tasha noted. "And now a second one just joined it."

"Yeah, that second one"—Mariana pointing to the other one on the screen, as she stood off to the side, "that one's Calum."

Terk looked at her in shock, and she shrugged. "I can hear his thoughts. He's approaching the person in front, and he can see him bending over a deceased body on the floor," she explained, her eyes closed. "Cal has his gun at the ready, and he's wondering ..." When she opened her eyes, all of them were staring at her. She shrugged. "What? You guys think you're the only ones who can do this shit?"

"Have you ever had the ability to do this before?" Terk was shocked at her demonstration, even though she'd told him about her ability to connect to Calum.

"It's not an ability, not in a learned sense," she replied. "My grandmother would have called it *the sight*. It just seems to be really strong whenever I feel close to Calum."

"That's because he has it too," Terk noted quietly.

She nodded. "I got that sense too early on. It was part of the reason why our relationship felt so right."

He smiled. "Because it *is* right, never doubt that."

And, with that, she laughed. "Maybe," and then she froze. "*Uh-oh*. I bet you've got another heat signature. Cal's hearing voices."

"We have two more approaching the house," Tasha confirmed, "but he shouldn't hear those voices."

Mariana frowned. "Well, he is. I'm not exactly sure if that's new or just different, but he is definitely hearing voices."

"Okay, people, on alert right now," Terk said. "We need faces. We need recognition. We need IDs. And we need to know who the hell is after Calum. And why they chose to kidnap Mariana."

"Well, the more she talks, the more we learn about how unique she is," Tasha noted. "Chances are she was targeted to draw him out, sure, but maybe also because of her own skills."

"It's possible," Terk agreed, "but somebody would have

to know about them first." He looked at Mariana, who shrugged and shook her head.

"Nope, I can't see that happening. My family were carnival nuts, and they ran a fortune-telling booth for a long time," she shared, "but I never ever worked it. It went against everything that I wanted in this world."

"So that is highly doubtful then. The trouble is, if anybody finds out now," Terk warned, "you *will* be targeted."

She stared at him in surprise and then slowly realized what he meant. "Fine, my lips are sealed."

Terk nodded. "Not for too long, I hope. We need to know if you see anything else."

"Definitely something is there," she said. "I just don't know whether it's of any value or not." And, with that, closing her eyes, she turned her attention to Calum. "He's hidden now." And then a weird slam came in her head. She opened her eyes, stared at everyone around her, in shock. "I think he just shut a door on me." She spun to look at Terk.

"Yeah, he would." He nodded. "That makes total sense, especially under times of stress like that. He can't afford to not be 100 percent focused. Any distraction right now could kill him."

"Got it." She frowned. "In that case I'll just deal with Little Calum and try to forget what Cal's doing."

"That would be good," Terk agreed. "But first, tell me this. When you told me that you used to do this as a kid, what exactly did you mean?"

"I used to kind of—I don't know—jump into people's thoughts, get what they were thinking somehow. Different than when you were sending me information after Cal got hurt because that deliberately came from you to me. It's more like overhearing what was happening with Merk. Then

I forgot about it because it was just a childhood game, until I met Cal. We had some sort of a connection, part of that whole 'meant to be together' thing that couples experience, but, like I said, ever since he got injured, it's been so much clearer and stronger between us."

"Do you think he knows?" Terk asked her.

"I don't know." She frowned. "If he doesn't know, it's because he's not looking at it."

"Maybe he's hearing voices or thoughts and doesn't know where they're coming from."

"Exactly, when, in actual fact, it's me."

"Okay." Terk nodded. "That's something else we must clarify when we get to it." And, with that, he turned his attention back to the computer.

CAL SLIPPED THROUGH to the back of the house. He'd heard something off, something registering in his peripheral vision, but he wasn't exactly sure what it was. Or maybe *peripheral hearing* was a better phrase, but he didn't know what to make of it. Ever since he'd woken up from the coma, things were different.

It's like he heard more noise going on in there, more of everything converging in his mind, but he hadn't mentioned anything to Terk. Cal made a mental note to talk to him about it, and he needed to do it soon. There really just hadn't been time. Terk was the man to talk to if you had problems with powers though. Terk's connection to the ether was stronger than all of them, sometimes to the point of making the team feel like a bit of a fool.

However, Calum should have come out of that coma

feeling better, not worse. But some things were just not working out the way they were supposed to. As long as he kept fighting it, he also knew he was fighting himself, and that wouldn't help any of them. He needed help.

Fighting on that level affected him—though in fairness, he couldn't remember everything, like specific things Terk had taught him. Those lessons had been very hard to grasp, but, once learned, they were not exactly something you would ever forget, but he had, and everything was coming to him in bits and pieces. He'd been coming in contact with the raw side of his powers, which wasn't something he had done before.

And even now he felt like he could do more, so much more to be honest. It was a matter of having the time to sort it out, not when they were under the gun with whatever asshole was after them right now. First things first, and that was keeping his family out of danger. Then he would figure out what was going on with his skills.

He almost heard a whisper in the back of his mind, but he shut it down, since it didn't pertain to what he was doing right now. It was more important that he keep everything flowing and moving in the direction it needed to move, instead of getting caught up in his head—which just led to the craziness of trying to figure out what was going on, when maybe it was nothing.

That kind of confusion was deadly. He slipped forward another few feet, wondering what he heard here, when suddenly a horrific noise sounded off in his ears. He clapped his hands over his head, wondering if some dog whistle or a high-pitched computer sound were intentionally going off.

He dropped to his knees, and almost instantly Terk slammed into his brain. He had wrapped something around

62

Cal's mind and was telling him to shut down.

Shut down right now!

Cal immediately broke all connections to everything, but with that came a horribly weird sense of disorientation.

Even in his coma, Cal had sensed something. Someone being there with him, someone he could connect with. Most of the time that had been Terk himself, and, if he were the one telling him to shut down, there wasn't a whole lot Calum could do about it except shut down.

He quickly slipped into a closet and huddled on the floor, waiting for the pain in his head to stop pounding. With his senses shut down, everything was distorted, disconnected. He knew from experience that it would last a few minutes, and that it would be harder to hear until he could adapt. But his shuffling from one to the other wasn't as good as it could be.

He felt somebody out there, somebody concerned and somebody with an eye on him. He figured it was Terk, but, having already delivered the message, Terk should know that Cal would be fine. But then, from Terk's point of view, Calum had just come out of a long period of recovery and probably wasn't thinking he was fine at all. It was a weird thing to consider that, to most of the team, he was operating at less than full capacity. Not exactly the way he wanted to go through life, and yet it's just what it was. The team knew better than to label it good or bad in a case like this; they knew this would just be their reality for now.

Taking a slow deep breath, Calum released it, letting the energy flow through him and out. And, sure enough, as soon as he completed that deep breath, everything started to realign. He took several more calming breaths, waiting for the present surroundings to return to his senses. And finally he could stand up and look around.

Don't know what that was, he muttered in his head, *but maybe it did what it was supposed to do.* Cal got no answer. He slowly took another look around. He'd stepped into an office. He'd found the body on the floor, with a single gunshot to the head. Even as he stood here, studying the layout, Cal sensed Damon crying out for him. Cal immediately took a few steps back and walked over to where he found Damon, with intense pain reflected on his friend's face. Cal held out a hand and pulled him to his feet. "Just close off that door," Cal relayed to Damon, telling him the same message Cal got from Terk.

"I did," Damon said, "but it still feels like something's in there."

"That's not good. Try it again, then give it a few minutes," Cal replied, then waited as his friend worked at it.

Finally Damon nodded. "Wow, I forgot what those boomers felt like."

"Let's hope we never get the opportunity to figure it out again," Calum stated quietly.

"We've already had some people using these things on us," Damon noted, "but honestly, I wasn't expecting it today. Guess I should have been."

Cal nodded. "We're not perfect, and, right now, we're less than even optimal, in fact, so let's not start laying blame or BS like that."

Damon gave him a sheepish grin. "I hear you. It just seems like, once again, everybody is operating in such a way that we don't have a clue what's happening, but the bad guys all do. It's always that way, until we get ahead of the curve," he muttered.

"All we're looking for is whoever the hell attacked us.

CALUM'S CONTACT

After that, we can figure out who the rest of these assholes are. Unfortunately, all we've been given are bits and pieces, leading us to more assholes. That's because they keep throwing up smoke screens to keep us off track," Cal added succinctly. "I don't know about you, but I'm kind of done with that whole tactic."

Immediately Damon nodded. "It's good to have you back, bud."

"I hear you," Cal replied. "It was pretty rough in that coma. I could hear all kinds of things and yet couldn't respond to any of them."

Damon looked at him in surprise. "Were you aware?"

"To a certain extent, yes. Don't ask me what I was aware of."

Damon nodded in understanding. "That's one of the harder things, isn't it? We are all just trying to sort out all those crazy impressions, and figuring out what everybody is trying to say and to do is almost impossible. Yet there's no real option, so it is what it is."

"Exactly." They slowly moved through the house. "How are we handling all the bodies we're finding?" he asked Damon.

"We've been dumping them on Merk and Jonas."

"Well, that's handy," Cal said.

"Honest to God, it has been. Very handy. I'm sure the locals think that Merk is leaving a swath of pain everywhere he goes right now, but honestly, it's us. Or not even us so much as these guys cleaning up behind themselves and killing their own people to prevent us from getting to them."

"Is that it?" Cal asked.

Damon nodded. "As far as we can tell, yes, … the assholes."

65

"Yeah, that was my thought too." Calum laughed. "But the bottom line is, we need to get as much intel as we can off this guy."

"Yeah, that's been our standard process," Damon agreed. "We'll take his photo and get shots of any ID on him. Then we'll send on all the information. He's just one more piece of the puzzle and was likely taken out because it was easier to kill him than keep him on and have to deal with anybody else opening their mouth."

"And we don't have anybody left who has opened their mouth, correct?"

"Correct," Damon replied quietly. "Took them out right in front of us a couple times."

"These guys are so busy killing everyone off. It's an interesting tactic and not the most common," he murmured, "though we've seen it before to some degree."

"Bodies still talk."

"I've always thought that too," Cal noted, "but you know? These guys don't seem to believe that same theory. Which is also odd, so who the hell is running that side of things that finds life of so little value? They can kill off somebody without a thought, and they don't mind hiring new people. New people take training, and, once the word gets out that nobody's left alive, how will they keep bringing in new hires?"

"I've been trying to figure that out myself," Damon admitted. "I came up blank because, seriously, who will sign onto a team that has no regard for life? The thing is, the ones we have been able to talk to—before they were also taken out—they had no idea that they too were expendable. I wonder if this guy had a clue."

They both moved into the office. "This is not Sean Calvert," Calum said. "This is his brother David."

"Well, shit," Damon replied. "Do you think Sean would have killed his brother?"

Cal frowned at that. "I don't know," Cal replied finally. "You know what? My first thought would be no, but I also don't understand a lot of what's going on right now. So, if I say no, I'd say it with that caveat in mind."

"How about we just keep it as is, as a no, until we can find out something further. But let's also look at a scenario where this guy is potentially capable of killing his brother, perhaps to keep him in line or even to make it look like you did it."

Calum winced at that. "That would be even more of a reason for Sean to kill David."

"Who is this Sean Calvert guy? Or, more important, why does he hate you so much? So much that he hates the rest of us too. And why would he want anyone to believe that you killed his brother?"

"It could be anything, Damon." Cal was not being unhelpful; he truly had no idea. "I've always worked instinctively, and anything could have pissed off Calvert," he explained in a short tone, with a bite to his voice. "The guy has hated me since we were in training together."

"Oh, crap, don't tell me that he was a US Navy SEAL?" Damon asked in shock. "A UK citizen?"

"Dual citizenship. And no he washed out," Cal told him. "That just added to the hate. He went on to become a mercenary, while I ended up doing what I set out to do. So, maybe from Sean's perspective, that was a triumph for me and a failure for him."

"Something that he really couldn't forgive you for."

"Well, I wondered about that, as soon as we realized that

Calvert was involved. But I mean, is that enough reason to hate him now? He may be a victim in all of this himself."

"I don't know. If it was advertised that you killed his brother, and he just found out about it, would that be enough to turn him on you? He already had a grudge against you."

"Yes, that would probably do it," he agreed.

"Do we know how long this guy has been dead?"

Cal studied the body; it wasn't necessarily fresh. There was no rigor, and the body was past cold. There was definitely an odd look to it, but, as far as decomp, he studied the room. "The house is cold."

"What's the first thing that comes to mind when you look at the body?" Damon asked Cal.

"I think—my take on this would be that he's been dead for at least a couple days now. And maybe that's what pushed Calvert into kidnapping Mariana, for revenge, you know? Thinking that I'd killed his brother."

"But wouldn't revenge just mean killing Mariana outright? And why wouldn't he have buried his brother? Intentionally leaving his brother here to be found like this, … that just doesn't sit right."

"I agree, unless Sean hoped to call the cops and let them find us here with the DB." Calum studied the scene. "I don't find any other energies descending upon us. Plus, let's get real. This guy wasn't killed here. There's no blood. Nothing says that he was killed on this property at all."

"So, you're thinking these guys killed him somewhere else? Then they showed Sean the body, just enough to get him stirred up and ready to take you out. Then came and delivered the body here for us to find."

"Jesus, that sounds a little on the implausible side, but I

don't have a better theory." Calum was unsure, but, at the same time, nothing else made sense either.

"It is ludicrous," Damon agreed. "But I don't know what else to say, so let's just keep on working our way through this." He took several photos of David's body, then sent them off to Terk. Now they searched the rest of the house.

"We need something that says more about this guy. Do we even know for sure whose house this is?"

"It's listed as Calvert's father's originally," Damon noted, "but it could easily have been the family home."

"Which would make some sense that this guy was left here."

"It would," Damon agreed slowly. "But you know what? As we go over this, none of it really makes sense. Does Calvert have that short a fuse where you're concerned?"

Calum stared at his friend and then slowly nodded. "Yes, you could say that."

"So, something else is going on?"

"I dated his sister for a while. She only dated me to get back at Sean, and I dated her because I thought she was cute," he added, with a wry smile. "It backfired on both of us. Calvert lost it big time when he found out, and she immediately took it out on me, I think to defuse her brother's anger, or maybe just to get back at me. I don't know. We broke up shortly thereafter, and we both agreed on that. However, she had an awful lot to say that wasn't terribly nice or true."

"And that probably set off Sean even more."

"Not that he needed a reason, but yes," Cal confirmed. "That set him off even more."

"Interesting. Somehow, when we get these oddball enemies, they fill our life with craziness, right?"

"What a pain in the ass," he stated bluntly. "I never did anything to him, but he's been hating on me for a very long time."

"And when you hate someone for that long ..." Damon added, "that's why we've got so many problems right now."

After a few moments of silence, Cal shook his head. "I just don't think he would have been behind all this."

Damon looked up in surprise. "So what are you thinking?"

"I just can't see it, and I don't think it's even possible. Sure, he may hate me, but this is his brother, and he just left him here?"

"I can't say I disagree," Damon replied, "and, Jesus, nothing here is really making sense anyway."

"No, I hear you. It's just one more of those puzzles that we have to get to the bottom of."

"Well, first we have to find this guy before he goes after Mariana again," Damon noted. "Sounds to me like she's pretty special if she can handle what you do."

"Yeah, but can she handle it long-term though?" Cal asked in a wry tone. "And my son, he's already been traumatized."

"Yet I saw him with you, and you all looked pretty happy," Damon replied.

"Turns out it was the best healing experience I've had in a while," Cal agreed, "or maybe ever. I'm still not convinced that it's fair to them, but I'm happy for them to be with me."

"That's great." Damon smiled.

"Maybe *fair* isn't the right word," Calum added, "but, if anything were to happen to them, you know how I'll feel. She talked about how important it is, when you have something going for you, to maximize the time that you have to enjoy it. So, maybe it's the right thing. I don't know. I'm confused at this point."

"Agreed, but we all just need some time to work it out."

"Well, that's the whole point of this." Cal nodded. "I want that time to work it out."

Damon's phone buzzed. "Speaking of time," Damon added, checking his cell phone's screen, "what do you say we do another search of this house and then we get moving. Gage is waiting in the truck and getting antsy. Feels we might get company soon."

"Agreed," Calum stated, "but where to next?"

"Well"—Damon stared at Cal—"you said that Calvert has a sister."

"And?"

"Maybe we should go talk to her. I already have Gage on point to find her."

Calum wasn't impressed at the prospect of having to deal with her, but, while they waited on an address for her, they did another check of the property. When the address was delivered to their phones, they noted it was only ten minutes away.

"That kind of makes sense too," Cal muttered. "She was very close to her family."

"All the family or just her brother?"

"Her parents," he clarified. "I'm not sure about David, this brother. I just don't know."

"Okay, let's go have a talk." And with everybody else on their side notified, they headed out to the vehicle. "Does Mariana know about the sister?"

"It was before her time, and it's never come up, so probably not," he said. "Is that something I'm supposed to tell her too?" His tone was dry. "All the rules of marriage get a little confusing sometimes."

"I think the only thing that's not confusing about it is that you're supposed to serve and to protect," Damon noted. "Kind of like the police."

Cal laughed. "I have definitely heard marriage described by some as a kind of captivity, but it was never that way for me. I just ..." Calum trailed off. "I've always been afraid that, someday, somebody would come and destroy everything that I had built."

"And it did happen in a way," Damon reminded Cal.

"It did, indeed, and now I don't know what to do."

"Well, you might want to remember that, although it happened, your family is safe. We did get them back, and now you have a second chance."

"One of the things that I came out of the coma with was the feeling that I'd already lost and wasted enough time. I need to make changes and to stop putting things off because other people are affected as well."

"I know what you mean," Damon said, trying to ease the situation. "That happened to all of us to some degree. For what it's worth, I've been trying not to think about it too much for now."

"It's a damn hardship for everybody."

"Yeah, well, let's hold this talk for a better time, and let's go see if we can find the sister."

"Right," Calum growled.

"What's her name? I'm looking forward to seeing her."

"Tay. ... And, for the record, I'm not looking forward to seeing her at all," Cal muttered. "When we parted, it wasn't good."

"Did you do anything to hurt her?"

"Nope, but her brother sure thought so."

"Well, it's time to have a talk with her then and see just how much of this crap is her versus him."

Calum winced. "That wouldn't make me feel very good either."

"Doesn't matter how it makes you feel at this point," Damon stated cheerfully. "Let's go."

CHAPTER 4

M ARIANA HAD HANDED off a list of things she could use, and, after two people had left, she wasn't even sure which one had disappeared with her list. She was on a fact-finding mission, but, for now, she needed to focus on her son.

"I guess there's no outdoor playground around here, is there?" The question was directed at Terk, who paused to look over at Little Calum. Mariana shrugged. "That would help him ease into this, although I don't think it's an issue today. He's pretty tired and stressed, but some fresh air would do him some good and would help him to forget faster."

Terk nodded. "You know what? Let me take a look into that." Then he turned his attention to his phone and quickly brought something up.

"It doesn't have to be today."

"No, but he would be better off, just like you said. It would help to distract him from everything that is happening and maybe help him sleep better tonight."

"Will tonight be an issue?" she asked hesitantly.

"I hope not," Terk replied, "but I can't tell you for sure that it won't be."

"You've always been very good at curtailing your answers that way."

He looked up at her in surprise. "Is that what I'm doing?"

"Well, you never really promise anything, and you never really give away anything, but, at the same time. you let it be known that, chances are, it'll be bad."

He laughed at what was a very accurate assessment of his words. "I hope not. I really don't want it to be bad at all."

"But?" A question was in her voice.

"It's possible. I don't know what we have coming."

"Or not coming …" she added.

"I presume, yes." He nodded. "Exactly. The thing is, you were found here in this building, right beside where we are living now. We are working on getting out of this building, but, at the moment, we haven't located the right property for us."

"What you are really thinking then," she noted quietly, "is that this will be the place of another attack."

"They didn't find us last time, but they did leave you and your son here, and obviously you weren't here when they came back, so odds are good that they know we must be nearby. We do have a smokescreen up around us," he added, "if that makes any sense."

She nodded slowly. "That makes a lot of sense. There was some discussion about it among my kidnappers at the time, as I recall." She frowned, trying to remember what she had overheard.

Terk waited, hoping she could remember something of value.

Finally she shook her head. "There was just … I don't know, like an expectation of something that didn't happen."

Terk nodded. "Not very helpful."

"So you … you're afraid that we're not safe here. Is that

it?" Mariana asked, though she wasn't sure she wanted to hear the truth.

"Let me just say I have my suspicions that another attack is likely."

"Are we leaving then?"

"No, we're not leaving." He shook his head. "And I guess that'll be a little hard for you to understand, but we have to make sure that what they're doing doesn't set us on the run every time."

"If you can protect this place," she noted, "then it makes sense to stay." He stared at her. She shrugged. "I can't say that I want to leave. But neither do I want to put my family in danger."

"Nobody wants to put your family in danger," he agreed. "Every one of us is committed to keeping you and your son safe. I understand that, from your position, it may not seem that way, and everything probably feels like a big mess." He shrugged, then continued. "But we've come a long way."

Mariana smiled. "I have no doubt about that," she murmured, "but I expect that probably an awful lot of people are working on stopping you from getting any further into this investigation."

He chuckled. "There's always that."

She nodded.

"It's always disheartening to discover that somebody out there is looking to bring down good people. I tend to look at them as being the type none of us ever need or want in our lives," Terk added. "And, because of that, you have to treat them in a totally different way."

"Okay, I can see that, but I bet the average person doesn't think this sounds so normal at all."

"Nothing about any of this is normal," he admitted, "but it's what we do. Now, for the moment, you're fine, and whatever we can do to make your lives a little easier is also good."

She hesitated, then nodded. "Like an outside space would be good. Little Calum will need something over the next few days to keep his mind off everything. This will work in the meantime, but I don't know how long we can stay here without some sunshine and fresh air."

"You'd be surprised," he replied, looking at her. "The guys could theoretically be just fine for weeks or maybe months."

"Are we likely to be here that long?" she asked, her heart sinking.

"No, I don't think so. Maybe a week or two though."

"Okay, I can work with that."

"But you can't hold me to it," Terk added, with a note of warning.

She grinned. "I get it. You really hate to lock down and define anything, don't you?"

"That's because the intel constantly changes, and we have to constantly change with it."

"Got it," she muttered, then shrugged. "So, what'll it be then?"

"In terms of what?" he asked, looking puzzled.

"In terms of my son. Is there a place around outside or no?"

"Yes." He gave her a knowing look. "But honestly, to me, it sounds like it's you who needs to get out, not him."

She sighed. "You know what? That's probably very true." She paused. "I guess I'm the one who's looking for something to do. Once I'd thought about taking him to a park, I found I quite liked the idea."

He nodded, then suggested, "I can go with you."

"No, you need to be here."

"I might be needed here," he confirmed, "but nobody is going out alone."

She groaned. "I hadn't considered that."

"Nope, I'm sure you hadn't. However, this is the way our team works. So it's me or no one leaves this building."

She looked over at the others. "Aren't you needed here?" She needed to get out, and Terk apparently understood her well. She hadn't ever been a part of their world, and she needed to be eased into their lifestyle.

"They're all just fine for a little bit," he replied. "Besides, I haven't been at a playground in forever." He gave her such a boyish look of hope that she burst out laughing.

"I can't believe that," she teased, "but, okay, the park it is." With that, she got up, bouncing to her feet to find Calum immediately.

"Park, park, park!" Little Calum cried out, overhearing that part.

Chuckling, she explained, "Just for a little bit though, okay? And you have to be good and listen to Mommy. When we say we're coming back, we're coming back, no arguments."

He nodded. "Park, park, park!"

She shook her head at Terk. "Fair warning, he won't be terribly keen about leaving once he's there."

"Can't say that I blame him." Terk suppressed his laughter.

"Easy for you to say," she replied. "As long as he gets an outlet for all that energy, he'll probably be fine." And, without a word, they headed out. The subtle things that

Terk did as they walked away had her confused. "What were you doing?" she asked, when they got outside.

"Closing up barriers, so nobody can go in when we're not there."

"So that keeps them all safe."

"Yes," he stated, without hesitation. "At least it keeps them as safe as possible under these circumstances."

"And if it doesn't?"

"The barrier will hold, but, if for some reason it doesn't, it will shoot off a warning for them. They won't be caught by surprise."

She swallowed and nodded. "I really do have to adjust my thinking."

"I'm sorry, but, yes. If you're planning on staying, then you're right. You do."

"Oh, don't you worry." She shot him a hard look. "I'm staying. If Cal is staying, so am I."

Terk nodded. "I understand. I get it, but it's not me you need to convince."

She realized he was right there. She would have to convince Cal. "I know …" She was determined to not be separated again. Outside, she stopped and searched the area. She felt a weird pressure in her chest as she looked around.

Terk was at her side. "It's fine," he murmured. He gave her a commiserating look. "The smokescreen separates us from the ones inside. It's protection for all of us."

"Is it though?" she asked, a hand at her chest and a worried expression on her face. "I just realized what I asked for."

He looked at her and then slowly nodded. "And I get that. You're not used to living with these odd sensations."

"Does anybody ever get used to it?" she asked.

He nodded comfortingly. "They do."

She pondered his words as they closely followed Little Calum around a corner, finding a parking lot and a small sandbox. He was jumping up and down the length of the lot and straightaway spotted a slide. "What was this originally?"

"The company that had this building years ago put in a daycare facility for the staff," he murmured.

"That's such a good idea," she noted. "Too often, the family unit gets broken up by the need to work, and there's almost no way to get back from the familial breakdown of the absenteeism when one of the members is away."

"And yet that's how most families function."

"Just because a few families function well that way doesn't mean it's for everyone," she argued.

He smiled at her. "I can see that in your face right now."

"You're quite right there."

He nodded. "Let Little Calum have a few minutes to enjoy this."

She noticed Terk's wording was a little off, but she didn't want to linger on it. She walked over and helped Little Calum into the swings and immediately started pushing him. She stood here for a long moment, just letting him enjoy the fresh air, talking and just taking it all in. They were having fun, and this was somewhat relaxing, maybe because it was a normal activity. She wasn't sure why she wasn't fully relaxed, but she was definitely aware of an odd sense to being out here right now.

She looked over at Terk to find him standing nearby but with an oddly watchful look on his face. She realized she really had pushed a lot of boundaries to get her son out here. *What had it taken for Terk to do this?*

She hoped he wasn't doing anything foolish because maybe they could have done something different. By the time Little Calum was all done with the swing, he moved on to the sandbox. She sat down on the 2x4 edge frame and helped him play.

When Little Calum got tired of that, he raced back over to the swing again. She stood, only to see Terk walking over and pushing him. He was laughing and loving it. She smiled at Terk, then sat back down. Terk just nodded with an oddly distant focus in his gaze.

She knew it wasn't the time to ask Terk more about this, so instead she watched them, as the guys kept busy at the swings. A few minutes later, Little Calum was back in the sandbox again. She was so happy to see so much excitement in his expression. He always loved activities, and to have a setting to play in had him bouncing up and down. She also knew that, as soon as they went back inside, he would ask to come back out here again over and over.

It was the nature of a child. Little Calum knew, if he asked long enough, it seemed like Mama always gave in. Even if not, there was always the hope that Mama would say yes next time. And he was certainly no different than any other kid. He had a lot of endurance when it came to getting what he wanted. More than she had in terms of resistance.

This was definitely not the time to be thinking about playdates. She had more immediate problems right now, so wasting an ounce of energy fussing about her parenting skills didn't make any sense. It took an hour and a half for Little Calum to wear down. As she looked over at Terk, she saw a certain amount of fatigue in his face. She gathered up the sweaty little boy and announced, "Okay, time to head back. It's nearly nap time."

"I'm hungry," Little Calum replied immediately.

"Good. In that case, food first, then nap time." They all

headed off together, and, as they got closer, Little Calum raced toward the door ahead of Terk. She looked at Terk and guessed, "You've been sending out some sort of a scrambling signal the whole time we've been out here, haven't you?"

His gaze, lidded and dark, just stared at her, the lights of his eyes flaring.

"There was ... this weird hum, on top of that coldness in my chest," she added. His gaze continued to deepen as he studied her. "I don't know what it is, but I do appreciate that you did this for us." And, with that, she turned and walked inside. She could have been ignorant before, but now she was trying to catch up. Not only was she sensing it, she was slowly understanding what was going on here.

She figured she had been correct when Terk didn't correct her. He didn't say a whole lot as they went inside the warehouse again, and, for that, she was grateful. She would have appreciated some answers—later—but she also wasn't really ready to deal with it right now.

Based on Terk's response, or lack of same, she figured he might seek her out later, and she was right. Little Calum ate his snack, but he had trouble eating more as he couldn't stay upright. Almost as soon as she had her son down for a nap, Terk was back, and he looked determined.

He motioned for her to leave their room, so they wouldn't disturb Little Calum while he was sleeping. Terk took her down to the end of the hall and then stopped to face her. "When you said you heard a hum, what did you mean?"

She looked at him, frowning. "Was I not supposed to hear a hum?"

"Nobody else has ever mentioned it," he stated calmly.

She was unsure what to say to him. "Well, maybe, ...

maybe nobody has the same level of hearing as I do. It just seems like, whenever you're doing your little security thingy, ... I hear something."

"My *little security thingy?*" he repeated, with a loud bark of laughter.

She smiled. "Well, I don't mean that in a disrespectful way."

"Of course not." He still chortled over her wording. "It's just that not many people would have termed it quite that way."

"I get that," she admitted. "I just don't know what else to call it."

"What you're calling it is just fine for now. So, how loud was the hum?"

"Minor," she replied instantly. "Just enough that I could recognize it."

He nodded slowly and thoughtfully. "It's odd that you heard it."

"I don't know why because I've told you that I do hear things sometimes."

He nodded. "It's definitely something for us to keep an eye on."

"You mean, the hum?"

"Yes," Terk said. "It would be much better if we don't give off any indicator at all of where we are. What you described is something that we cannot afford to have out there, announcing our presence. We don't want to tip anybody off."

She frowned, as she thought about it. "Are you saying that, because you've never had anybody tell you there's a hum, you didn't know there was one?"

"Correct," he nodded.

"*Hmm*," she muttered. "I can't really help you there because all I can tell you is that's what I heard."

"Well, if you ever hear anything different," he added, "let me know."

"Will do," she cheerfully said, as they both returned to her room. As she stopped at the doorway, she hesitated. "Are you guys okay if I go lie down for a bit?"

"Go." He waved a hand. "I'll clean up the kitchen."

She winced. "Oh, God, I didn't even think of the mess we made with Little Calum's snack. Sorry, my thoughts are so scattered, and I'm all over the place," She was heading back to the kitchen, but he gently pulled her back.

"Go look after your son. You're not alone here," Terk reminded her. "You have a team to back you up now."

She smiled at that. "Thank you. Help has been a little thin and far between in my world, so thank you for this. For all of it." And, with that, she returned to her room. As she opened the door, Little Calum was still happily crashed on the bed. She curled up beside him. *Sleep tight, baby, sleep tight.*

She almost heard him whispering against her ear, something soft about Daddy.

She hugged him tightly. "Daddy is fine. He will be here when you wake up," she whispered.

He'll be here soon.

She had no idea how, but she had touched Little Calum's mind and had eased his worries, and he drifted off into a deeper sleep. Only as her own eyes drifted closed, she realized she hadn't had an update from Terk on Cal's whereabouts.

She frowned, wondering if she should get back up and ask him. But then Little Calum shifted and wrapped his arm around her. Almost as if he understood what she was thinking, he whispered for her to stay.

"You staying here, Mommy?"

"I'm staying here," she replied immediately. And, with that, she thought, he finally would go under. Yet he was still restless the whole time. Although the park had been a good break, it would take much longer for Little Calum to get over that sense of doomsday. She wrapped her arms around him and held him close. She needed rest too, so she closed her eyes, and eventually she slept.

WHEN THE FRONT door to the house opened, the woman on the other side stared at Calum for a moment in shock, and then a fury like he'd never seen before lit up her face. Tay reached up and smacked Cal hard across the cheek. His hand went to his skin, now burning hot, and he stared at her for a long moment, before speaking. "What was that for?" he snapped.

"For my brother, you asshole," she yelled. "I had no idea you would bring so much grief to my family. I wish I'd never seen you before in my life."

"The feeling is mutual," he stated, "considering your brother kidnapped my family."

She stared at him and shook her head. "I don't know what you're talking about. All lies!" Her gaze flicked over to Damon. Her somewhat subdued resentment turned to fury again. She waved her hand at Damon now. "Another one of your assholes, here to do your bidding?"

"Not likely," Damon replied, studying her carefully. "I'm not sure why you're so angry at Cal, but I had nothing to do with it."

At that, Cal looked at his buddy in surprise.

"Don't know if this is personal or not, but honestly? Any woman who'll swing her hand at somebody she hasn't seen in a very long time obviously has some pretty hard feelings." Damon was careful not to piss her off too much. They needed information.

"You killed my brother," she yelled bitterly.

At that, both men stopped and stared, and, finally getting it, Cal immediately shook his head. "I did not kill your brother David," he stated carefully. "We just found him."

Tay openly stared at both men. "What do you mean, you just found him?"

"He was at Sean's father's house—or maybe it's someone else's house, but the deed is under his name."

"No, he's not. David's at the morgue."

"Really?" Damon looked from her to Calum.

"How do you know this?" Cal asked.

"Who told you that?" Damon followed up, when Calum got no response.

"I was just told about his death." She frowned.

Calum tried to sound sensitive. "Tay, just calm down and listen. David's body is still at Sean's father's house, and, from the looks of it, he probably died several days ago," he explained in a careful tone. She was just as likely to go off on another rampage, as soon as the words processed.

"That's bullshit," she yelled immediately. "That is absolute bullshit."

"Doesn't mean it's not true." Damon pulled out his phone and held up the pictures he had taken.

She stared at him. "Why is he there?" She was visibly shaken. "No, no," she shrieked. "Why would you take pictures of him like that?" She was hysterical. "There's no reason for him to be there."

"Well, he is," Cal repeated, "and I'm not exactly sure what's going on here, but I'm damn tired of your family playing games with mine."

She looked at him, bewildered. "No. ... This is all wrong."

"Oh, you're right about that," he snapped, his own voice turning hard. "Like I said, I'm not prepared to listen to any more of your lies. I want to know where your brother Sean is, so I can stop him from kidnapping my family again."

She shook her head at him.

Maybe this was a bad idea after all.

"I don't even know what you're talking about."

"No, of course not," Cal snapped. "Tell me that you didn't know that Sean took Mariana and my son and held them captive for twenty-four hours."

She shook her head slowly at his accusations. When she finally regrouped, she retorted, "I didn't even know you were married."

"Because it's none of your goddamn business. We broke up many years ago. So I don't give a shit what you know or not, but your brother knew. Your brother targeted them, for Christ's sake. My son is four years old, Tay. Think about it."

She shook her head again. "No, Sean wouldn't do that," she argued earnestly. "He would never do that."

"Keep telling yourself that," Calum stated in a low and deadly tone, still fuming. "You know how much he hates me."

"Sure he hates you because you killed our brother."

"No, Tay. He has hated me ever since you and I went out, maybe even before that. Jesus, talk about not wanting to revisit any of the same old lessons again," he muttered, with a bitterness he didn't even realize he was still holding so deep. "He has done nothing but hurt my family with his brutal arrogance."

She shook her head. "No, I'm not listening to you. It's not true."

"Which part? That he doesn't have anything against me or that he doesn't hurt innocent women and children?"

Then she snorted. "Of course he doesn't." Then she dropped all pretense and took on a catty tone. "Perhaps they're not so innocent."

At that, Calum stepped forward, looking ferocious and towering over her, until she backed up to the wall. Then he whispered, "Now would be the time to stop talking and to start listening." His eyes were bloodshot with rage. "You'll stop the bullshit right now and shut your trap." He glared at her, noting her silence. *Finally.* "I get that you don't want to listen to anything against your brother Sean because the two of you have always been so close, but don't go making the mistake of hurting my family. That is something I will not tolerate. I draw the line there, and I will not take that kind of abuse from you two without dishing out consequences you won't like."

He stepped back, as she watched his gaze like a hawk, her hands flittering around her face. "Okay, okay, I'm sorry. My last comment was uncalled for. I shouldn't have said it."

"You think?" He watched her even closer. "Your family has the ethics and morals of a snake oil salesman, so how the hell would you expect your brother to tell the truth?"

"He doesn't lie to me," she stated stiffly.

"Yeah? Well, it'll be interesting to hear what he has to say when you ask him what happened to my family."

She shook her head. "I'm not asking him that."

"Because you already know it's true," he confirmed bitterly. "But what do you care, as long as you get your pound of flesh out of me?"

She was fuming again now. "You know how he is."

"I don't even know what the hell your problem was and why you turned him on me in the first place."

Her face closed up at that.

"Oh, so you do remember." He deliberately made himself bigger and more imposing.

"Is that why you're here now?" she asked, her tone suddenly distant.

"The only reason I'm here now," he replied, "is because I need your brother to back the hell off. You people are way over the line, and I'm not having it."

"I haven't done anything," she snapped.

"Not so fast. You're looking just as involved as anyone else, so we might as well take you down at the same time."

She stared at him. "I would never do something like that."

"And that's just BS. I don't know much about you anymore, Tay," he murmured, "but it was pretty clear, after we split, that I didn't know a whole hell of a lot about you. Then, once you set your brother on me, all bets were off."

"I didn't do anything," she argued. "I just told him that we broke up."

"Yeah, and what was the reason you gave him? Don't bother to answer if you'll just lie."

She flushed.

He nodded "Exactly. You lie. Sean lies. No wonder you two are close. You literally sent him after me, and he's been after me ever since. I didn't even do anything to you. And now that your youngest brother is dead, you two are blaming me because it gives Sean further license to come after me all over again, which is all he's ever been looking for. Your psycho brother is nuts, and I can't believe we're still dealing with hurt feelings, after all this time."

"Come on. Sean's not that bad. He's just an overprotective brother."

"Lady, you haven't even seen overprotective," Cal growled, his fury building again. "He went after my son!" he yelled, the fury slowly rebuilding inside him.

She backed up, holding her hands out in front of her now. "Hang on. … Just calm down. He wouldn't have done that."

"Keep telling yourself that, Tay," he yelled, through his own red haze. He sensed Damon's concern at his side and pulled back, working hard to contain the rage and frustration that even now overwhelmed him. "Where is your brother?"

"Why would I tell you?" she asked, coming back more forcefully now. "So you can kill him too? You already cost me one brother." She shook her head. "I think not. I don't know what the hell is going on between the two of you, but you can leave me out of it."

"That ain't happening," Cal stated. "You involved yourself when you sicced him on me to begin with. And you don't even have the guts to tell me what you did." Calum's blood was boiling.

"I didn't do anything, at least nothing bad."

He just stared at her, his mood more ominous by the moment.

"Oh, fine," she huffed. "I told him that we weren't compatible and that you told me how you didn't want anything to do with me."

"Well, that's mostly right," he replied. "However, as you damn well know, it was mutual, and we both decided that we weren't good together."

"I know, but I didn't tell him that part," she admitted.

He stared at her. "And?"

"Well, I had to tell him something."

"So, … instead of telling him the truth that we both decided to call it off, I suppose you came up with some *extra* reason that you haven't told me yet?"

"I just said that we weren't compatible. And that you, … that you found somebody else," she added reluctantly.

"That's great, Tay. Thanks a lot," he replied in a harsh voice. "And years later, he's still after me? I don't know what the hell has gone on with your brother, but Sean's off the reservation now and pulling all kinds of shit. All because he's supposedly *justifiably* angry at me."

She flushed. "So I might have exaggerated slightly. I was pretty upset."

"Upset?" He stared at her in surprise. "Remember that part about it being a mutual decision?"

"Yes, but, at some point, I realized that I didn't want to lose you," she explained. "So, as much as it was a mutual decision, it was mutual on *your* part."

He shook his head. "No way. That's bullshit. You didn't want anything to do with me."

"Sure I did," she agreed. "I just wanted you to stay home."

"Which we talked about, and, under those circumstances, you didn't want anything more to do with me," he snapped. "We made a mutual decision to move on, and somehow you've managed to turn this into something that Sean feels he needs to go after me for. And he has been looking for a reason to do that ever since."

She flushed at that. "He has always been overprotective," she repeated, "but he would never do anything to hurt children."

Calum stared at her, saying nothing, but he walked closer to her, his fist clenching and unclenching.

"He really kidnapped them?" she asked hesitantly, her gaze going back and forth from one guy to the other.

Both men nodded.

"Jesus, I don't even know what any of this means now."

"It means that your brother needs to be stopped. He also was overheard saying it was something that wouldn't make me very happy, and he was delighted to do that."

She winced. "Well, you know how he feels about you. And that started before we even met."

"Yeah, so you just added fuel to fire and for no other reason than pure spite. Thanks for that." He tried not to show his pain over the betrayal. "I'll be sure to let my kid know how nice the rest of the world is."

"That's not fair," she said. Then she stopped and shrugged. "Okay, so I was hurt. Maybe I shouldn't have said anything to Sean."

"*Really?*" he snapped. "So even now you can't own up and tell the truth?"

"What the hell is wrong with you?" Damon asked her, and the interruption made her mad.

She got angry so quickly that she looked ready to attack.

"Yeah, there's the real woman coming out," Cal taunted, trying to antagonize her. "That didn't take very long, did it?"

"Oh, stop with the drama, and I'm sure your damn kid is just fine."

"Why would you assume that?"

She just glared at him.

Then suddenly he got it. "Jesus! Here I was prepared to believe that you had nothing to do with it, but, by your own admission"—he stared at her in horror—"you were a part of it!"

"No, I wasn't," she snapped but took a step back.

"Yes, you were. Good God, Tay, what the hell are you doing? Is this who you are now? I can't believe you're involved in attacking a child. That is really something to be proud of," he snapped. "But I just don't get it. You always wanted kids."

"Yes! I wanted *your* kids," she shrieked and starting sobbing.

He was dumbstruck and didn't even know how to respond to that. He turned to look at Damon, who stared at the woman in front of them like she was some kind of insect.

"So, am I to understand," Cal stated, trying to proceed cautiously, "that your participation was to target my kid for harm because he wasn't yours?"

She flushed and immediately shook her head. "No, no, no. Of course not."

But her denial wasn't coming across in a way that was believable. "Jesus. Don't say another word—or I swear I will hit a woman for the first time in my life," he growled out, holding up one finger in front of her. He obviously was trying to calm his breathing and to relieve the knot that had formed in his chest.

"What is this world coming to? What have *you* come to? Look. I'm not sure what the hell you've told yourself in order to make you believe this was okay. Or maybe you're just the kind of person who doesn't give a shit who gets hurt. But this is about my son, and I am not backing down. The idea that, since he's not yours, he can just be a victim that you don't really give a shit about, doesn't sit straight with me."

He continued to study her, while still reeling, as he struggled to reconcile this with the woman he had known, not that many years back. But it seemed like forever ago, which it was, since Cal had been married for six years now.

"You know what? When I came here, I figured you might know where your brother was, but I never even once considered that you were a part of the kidnapping of my family. How wrong could somebody be? God, you are nothing like the person I thought you were. Not back then. Certainly not now."

Cal turned to look at his buddy. "See, Damon? Can you imagine that *this* is what I went out with? I really dodged a bullet with this one." He shot another look at her, seeing the consternation on her face, along with the lingering denial, but, at the same time, he finally noted a hint of regret in her eyes.

"At least you have the decency to feel *some* shame for your actions," he snapped bitterly. "But unfortunately my son will carry the traumatic memory of this with him forever, all because of you and Sean." Turning to Damon, Cal said, "We might as well leave. She's complicit, so she's useless."

"What are you talking about?" she asked. "Nothing happened."

"You are as guilty as Sean is, so don't think for a moment that we'll go easy on you. Do you expect that the police will condone the kidnapping of innocent women and children?" Cal stared her down once again. "Are you really that naïve?"

"Nothing was supposed to hurt them," she yelled. "Sean told me that he would just use them as a warning."

"As a *warning*? That's great. For Christ's sake, your brother David got himself killed because he was working with Sean. Are you that stupid?"

"No, he wasn't," she argued. "David didn't want anything to do with Sean at all. He said our ideas were just stupid and that we'd get him in trouble."

"*Some trouble* all right. David's *dead*," Cal agreed. "Sean has obviously gotten in with the wrong crowd."

"If he was, I knew nothing about it."

Cal shook his head and backed up. "You'll have to talk to her, Damon. I can't stand to see her face." Then he turned and walked away.

"Wait," she called out. "Wait!"

But he kept on walking. He was sick to his stomach and so angry that he wanted to kill her. He had never hit a woman, much less killed one. Nothing else explained the burning rage inside his heart other than a deep hatred, a horrid betrayal, a painful worry about the psychological harm to his son, to his wife.

Tay ran after him and grabbed him by the arm, pulling him around.

He looked down at her, his fists clenched tight. "What?" he yelled.

"I'm sorry. I knew about the plan. I didn't exactly condone it," she explained, "but I didn't stop it."

"Why? You thought it would be funny or what?" he asked, with a mocking tone.

She flushed at that. "I didn't think. That's all. I just didn't think. I heard you were—" She blew out a long breath. "He told me that you had married and that you had a child, which was everything I wanted," she snapped. She paused to breathe again. "I just got angry, blind angry, and I didn't think. I didn't really consider it would even happen. Sean was just talking about it."

"Of course he was *just talking about it*," Cal growled. "Sean talks about everything. As you very well know." He smiled ruefully. "And, by the way, I didn't quit doing what I'm doing," he added. "I found the perfect woman, who didn't judge me for it instead." And, with that, he turned and walked away.

Cal knew that Damon would get whatever information there was to get from that piece of shit. At the same time, Cal was busy sending off signals to Terk to ensure that Mariana and Little Calum were safe. When he got Terk's message that they were both sound asleep and were fine, Cal eased back some of the panic in his chest.

As he looked over at Damon, he was in a heated discussion with Tay. Feeling better knowing Mariana and Little Calum were safe, Cal walked back toward them.

"I don't know where he is," she told Damon. "Sean comes and goes. And he's been really lost ever since our brother died."

"Ever since *you and Sean* killed David," Calum added from a few feet away.

She glared at him. "You're back?"

"Not because I want to be near you," he snapped, "but, if you think that you're not responsible for your brother's death, you're wrong about that too."

She yelled at him, "I had nothing to do with it."

"You really don't get it, do you?" Cal yelled back. "You'll lose *both* brothers now. The people Sean is involved with clean up behind them, and everybody involved—*everybody* who even knows them, like you—has been taken out as collateral damage to keep the lid on their organization and their methods. That way nobody knows what the hell these guys are up to. Bodies are dropping in their wake, quick and fast."

She swallowed hard. "What are you talking about? Sean isn't up to anything." But it was obvious that she was starting to lose faith in her own words.

He stared at her. "Either you tell us where he is, so we can arrest him—or you don't, and he is killed by whomever he's working with. If you won't tell us the truth, *even now*, we're wasting our time." He looked at Damon. "Let's just go."

"No, wait," she cried out in horror. "That's not fair."

"What do you know about fair?" he snapped, spinning on her.

She immediately stepped back, holding up her hands. "Look. That's not quite the right wording I was looking for. I don't know what's going on. I don't know what Sean's involved in. I don't think it has anything to do with my brother David's death, but I don't know."

"Of course you don't!" Calum was on the verge of breaking down. He was so out of patience and so out of time that he was just waiting for Damon to make the decision as to how to handle this crap. As far as Cal was concerned, they needed to just walk away and get going. He turned to Damon. "We can't waste any more time on her. We have to find her brother."

"What will you do when you find him?" she asked fearfully.

He looked at her. "What do you think I should do?"

She swallowed. "Look. He has never been a clear thinker where you're concerned."

At that, he stared at her. "And that's my fault?" he asked,

raising an eyebrow. "Seems to me you have an awful lot here you need to take responsibility for." Trying to shame her was the only way he saw to make progress.

She shook her head. "I don't know what's wrong with him. Recently, whenever I see him, he talks about some new business partners and says he'll make a ton of money, and, after all this is over, you'll remember his name."

"Me specifically or the world?"

"Probably both, but you for sure."

"Oh, I will. In fact, I remember his name already," he murmured. "No worries about that."

"Who are these people?" Damon asked her.

"He didn't tell me," she replied instantly.

Damon just stared at her.

"No, really. He just told me that I was better off not knowing."

At that, Cal looked at her, frowning, getting furious all over again. "And that didn't set off any alarm bells?"

"It did, and I asked him about it. Then I told him not to get mixed up in anything stupid."

"Really? This is Sean we're talking about," Calum snapped, incredulous.

She nodded. "I get that he has been a bit of a screw-up in many ways, but he does love me, and that's worth a lot."

Cal raised both hands and shook his head, turning away from her. He was trying hard to be understanding, but it was pretty damn difficult not to lash out.

"If you don't know who these people are," Damon asked, "you need to tell us where Sean is. Otherwise I can guarantee you that he's coming home in a box."

She stared at him in shocked silence.

Damon nodded. "You still don't get it, but these people

aren't playing. And what they did to Calum's family was just the start. They have a reason to come after us. They're trying hard to flush us all out and take us down. Permanently. Your brother really stepped up and helped them find us by kidnapping Cal's family. But hear me when I say this, they don't leave witnesses."

She looked over at Calum and then nodded. "I can see that. Calum was always protective."

"I still am," he snapped bitterly, "and believe me. It's eating at me that my wife went through what she did, as well as my son. The thought that you had anything to do with it? ... God, you are heartless." He shook his head, as he stepped back, feeling the fury overwhelming him again.

With fisted hands, he raised his voice and told her, "Stay the hell away from me and my family. The next time I see you, I will kill you—unless these guys get to you first. I promise you that." He needed to work on his control in a big way, but, right now, that was a little beyond him. He put it down to lack of energy.

"I'm sorry," she replied abruptly.

Damon looked at her expectantly. "Where's Sean?"

She nodded. "I get it. Look. I don't know where he is."

"What's his phone number?" Cal asked abruptly. She frowned and hesitated. "Seriously?" he said. "If there was one thing you could look back on and wish that you had changed, it'll be this moment in time. I can't guarantee that we can save your brother, and chances are, it's already too late."

"Wait. It shouldn't be," she argued, then pulled out her phone and quickly sent a text to her brother. "I've contacted him," she said, waving her phone. "I don't know where he is, but maybe he'll tell me."

"And maybe he's past being able to tell you," Cal stated.

"I don't think so. He was looking forward to seeing you."

Cal snorted at that. "Yeah, I'm looking forward to seeing him too. Which one of us has the better motivation?"

She flushed. "Please don't kill him," she said fearfully. "He's the only one I have left."

"Might have been nice if you had thought about that before you sent Sean down this pathway," Cal stated, trying hard not to let the bitterness overwhelm him.

She winced. "Look. I'm grateful that nothing bad happened to your son," she added, "but please don't kill my brother."

He shook his head. "No promises."

When she got a responding text, she smiled. "See? He's fine. He answered me."

"Yeah? And what did he say?"

"He says he'll be home soon." She shrugged. "I still don't know where he is though."

"Ask him."

She quickly sent another text message, asking where he was. Her phone rang almost immediately, and, as she picked it up, she put it on Speakerphone. "Where are you?"

"I am here. How is he? Is he really there?" At that, she looked over at Calum and Damon fearfully. "He appears to be fine," she replied unsurely, but Calum cut her off.

"You're damn right I'm here, and you can bet I'm not going anywhere until I get to the bottom of this." Calum was bitter. The call was disconnected after that.

When her phone rang again, she answered it, this time not on Speakerphone. "Yes, Calum is here, standing right in front of me. And he's really pissed."

"Of course he's pissed." Her brother's voice carried, sounding almost joyful over the phone. "Hold tight. I'll be right there." And, with that, he hung up.

She looked over at them. "He says he's on his way."

"Glad to hear it. We can have this out, once and for all."

She winced. "You did hear my request, right?"

"Oh, it won't be me who kills him," Cal explained. "I might take him in for a little *questioning*," he added in a not-so-subtle tone.

She flushed. "He's not a bad guy."

"He didn't used to be. I'll give you that," Calum confirmed. "But, ever since he didn't make it through navy training and washed out, he hasn't been the same. You of all people should know that by now. He's not stable, Tay."

"That was years ago." Tay stared at them. "And being used as a pawn in some game like this, that's BS. And I get it." She showed her palms. "I am partially responsible for your trouble with him. I'm sorry for that."

He just shook his head.

"I mean it," she said. "I wasn't thinking, and I just reacted. I was trying to get him off my case for dating you in the first place, for one thing. I thought it'd be funny to turn that attention toward you."

At that, he lifted his gaze and stared at her. "Do you think kidnapping small children is funny?"

She took a deep breath. "Well, in that case, maybe I just didn't think."

Enough bitterness was in her voice to make them both look at her.

"I thought I'd be married and have my own kids by now," she stated, "and instead I don't even have a long-term relationship."

Cal shook his head and didn't respond.

"I get that it's my own fault, and I probably deserve anything you say. I just ... I didn't think."

"Not only did you not think but you also didn't really utilize common sense. Just contemplate what you allowed to happen to a child. Maybe it's a good thing you don't have any," Cal stated brutally. She stared at him in such a wounded way that he felt terrible immediately. But that passed as he now knew what she had done to his family. And, for that, it would be damn hard to forgive her. He looked around, studying the area. "What direction does he come in from?"

She hesitated, and he just gave her that disgusted look. She frowned. "He has a parking spot out back."

"So, is he living here with you?" he asked in surprise.

She nodded slowly. "Yes, but just for the last couple days though."

"And you still aren't thinking straight. Your other brother, David, what did he do for a living?"

"He was in IT. Sean approached him about doing some work for these same people, but David didn't like anything about the deal."

"Smart man," Cal replied. "That explains why David is dead."

"What do you mean?" she asked.

"These people have already killed several IT people who were working for them."

She made a strangled exclamation.

"We both already told you that they kill everybody," Damon stated in a harsh tone, shaking his head.

Calum added, "We're not kidding. These people are playing for keeps."

And she froze. "That's plain murder. It's not even allowed."

"Nobody gives a shit about what's allowed," Cal yelled, shaking his head. "You weren't naïve before, so don't be stupid about it now. They've been killing off all their IT people—and anybody else in their employ."

"But David didn't work for them, so why would they have killed him?"

"Did your brother Sean ever show David any of other IT work done for these guys to see if David would be interested?"

She nodded. "Yes, Sean told David everything."

"Well, that explains why they killed David first out of the three of you," Calum noted.

"So, where does he come in? What door?" Damon was getting alarmed.

She motioned toward the back. "He'll be coming in through the back door."

"And why is he living with you again?"

She flushed. "Because he hasn't been able to get a stable job. And, when he does, it's mostly interim contracts. Then too, he blows the money on booze. It's not very nice living with somebody who's a drinker. David warned me about getting out before it got bad, but, well, I didn't."

"Well, hopefully for your sake, you'll have enough money that you can move on and get a life of your own," Cal suggested, feeling some of his anger drain away.

"Living like this, obsessed with the past, isn't good. I get it," she admitted. "I just didn't realize how much I was being influenced, but I can see it now." She straightened her shoulders. "I'll do better. I promise."

Cal replied, "Don't make promises to me that you can't

keep." He then looked over at Damon.

"I'll watch the back," he confirmed.

"Good idea," Calum replied. "I'll stay here and make sure she doesn't send out any alerts."

She stared at him. "Who would I even alert?" she asked. "You don't understand, Cal. It's just been the two of us for a very long time."

"And David, your *other* brother?" he asked, noticing her odd wording.

She flushed. "David hasn't had a whole lot of respect for either of us for quite a while. Honestly, I won't be at all surprised if we're not even in his will."

"Where is Sean?"

"I don't know what happened to him." She stared around her fearfully. "Now you've got me looking over my shoulder."

"So you should," Cal stated, "because, when we said these guys Sean is involved with weren't leaving anybody alive to tell the tale, we meant *nobody*. Just like your brother David was shot. Execution style."

She gasped and shook her head. "Sean wouldn't let them do that."

"That's because you assume they'll leave Sean and you alive too."

At her second gasp of horror, Damon bolted around to the back of the house.

CHAPTER 5

MARIANA WOKE UP with a start and sat upright. Thankfully Little Calum wasn't still in her arms. Sometime, while sleeping, he'd shifted over. She hopped to her feet, checked that he was fine, and bolted from the room. She raced down the hall toward the main working quarters. A meeting was in session, but Terk immediately stood at her approach.

"What's the matter?" he asked, as she took several deep breaths, trying to calm her racing heart.

"Is he okay?" she cried out. "Is he?" Terk looked at her. "As far as I know, yes. What are you getting?"

She kept shaking her head. "He's in danger. I know it. I am telling you, Terk. Cal's definitely in danger."

"I get that," Terk noted. "Sometimes they're in danger a lot." His voice was calming but alert, as a word of warning.

"No! Not like this. *Not like this. … Not like this.*" She couldn't get the words out. "Somebody … *It's a trap.* Somebody is trying to kill him." The others stared at her, while Terk, instead of arguing, got a really odd look on his face and froze.

She walked around him in a big circle. Then she looked over at the audience around the control room. "Does anybody have any contact with Cal?"

"I'll reach out to Damon right now." Tasha sent out a

text. "They're waiting for Sean to show up," she shared a moment later. "So far no sign of him."

"Warn them," Mariana snapped. "Warn them it's a trap. More than one's coming."

Tasha studied her, even as she dialed. As soon as Damon answered the phone, Tasha explained what Mariana was getting for a message.

"That would fit." And he hung up.

"They are duly warned," she stated, looking over at Mariana. "Damon confirmed how that would fit, and then he hung up. But at least they're warned."

Mariana nodded, her hands shaky.

Sophia immediately stood, then walked over and grabbed her hands. "You've done the best you can. Now trust them. Now you need to be strong. Let me get you some coffee." Quickly she raced over to the coffeepot, brought back a full cup, and handed it over. "Try to calm down."

"How do you guys do this?" Mariana asked, whispering.

"We do what we can do," Tasha murmured. "We help where we can help, and, when we can't help, we step back and let them do what they do. Our guys are real pros."

Mariana smiled at that. "Thank you, I needed that reminder."

"Good. You're not the only one who started getting some connection with these guys, but ours is obviously not as defined as the connection you have with Cal. We would like ours to be that way though, stronger."

Tasha nodded. "I don't know what changed," she noted. "It happened when Damon was in the coma. Before that, I always felt a little bit of a connection. I could kind of check in mentally and see that he was fine, and that was good enough for the longest time. But then, when he was not fine"—she paused—"when he was in the coma, I utilized that time to constantly check in because I was so worried about him." She sighed, showing her palms.

"How can you not be worried about them?" Mariana rambled, in shock now, and everyone just let her be. "I was always waiting for the day he'd come back and say he was retired and good to go. I knew that he was getting out of the industry because I'd heard this was all being shut down, so I was expecting to hear from him."

Mariana shook her head. "The days went by, and I didn't hear anything at all. Then, when Terk told me what had happened, I just went to pieces. And—somewhere along the line, in the midst of one of those long lonely nights—while I was silently searching and crying out for him, I connected. And ever since then, I just, well, ... I haven't let go," she admitted. "Cal probably won't like it, but I just ... I can't let go."

"I'm not saying that's right or wrong," Sophia noted, "but maybe relax a bit, so it's not quite so intense as it may seem to him. These guys all appear to have a problem when women are possessive."

"It's not coming from a possessive place at all," she explained. "It's intuitive. It's just a very close connection. I don't want to let it go because, well, it just feels right."

"Then don't," Tasha stated, as she walked closer. "If it feels right, just go with it. So much of what Terk teaches is intuition and learning to understand and to honor the feelings that you have. So don't let go, stick close, and maybe we can use your ability to help us."

"It's not really an ability," Mariana argued. "It's just ..." She didn't know what to say. Finally she shrugged. "Honestly, I would just call it love."

Tasha gave her the most beautiful smile she'd ever seen. "There is no such thing as *just* love. It's a huge gift, Mariana."

"And whether he understands it or not," Terk pitched in, "the point right now is that it's giving you a connection to him that you didn't have otherwise, which could be very valuable in terms of keeping him safe while we get through this."

She held her cup of coffee tightly, as she looked around at Tasha and Sophia and Lorelei. "Did you guys ever think about what you'll do afterward?"

All three nodded.

"I think in my case," Tasha shared, "Damon wants to continue doing similar work. So I'd work with him as I always have. There is talk about setting up the team as an independent entity," she said, watching Mariana carefully, "but we've not had a formal meeting about it."

Sophia added, "Same here." Lorelei nodded and smiled.

"It's very difficult for those of us who are left behind and waiting." Mariana struggled to share her true feelings. "If I was involved in some way," she noted, "I wouldn't be sitting around waiting and worrying, ... but it could also be dangerous for my son, and that would be hard."

Recognizing her need to talk, Tasha sat quietly and let her work it out.

"Yet we saw how well *living separately to protect us* worked out," she snapped, sounding deliberately sarcastic. "But, if we can't even walk away from the danger, then what's the point of thinking that we'll ever be safe in any way, shape or form?"

The other women laughed, which Mariana didn't understand.

"We hear you," Sophia confirmed, "but it's not us who you have to convince. It's Cal. After this, who knows if you'll manage to do that or not. You've both been through a lot."

"Unless I can find something I could do to make it seem like I'm helping the team," she suggested.

"Well, these guys, at first, see that as us running to the danger, instead of away from it," Sophia explained, chuckling. "But, after they see what we have to offer them, they eventually agree. Particularly since everybody is working so hard to keep them safe."

"So, if I get more warnings like this, I should be passing them on, right?"

"Absolutely," Terk stated, from behind her. He smiled gently. "Any time you get something like that in your head, we definitely need to know."

She nodded. "Are you against women joining the team?"

He stared at her in surprise, pointing around the room to Tasha, Lorelei, and Sophia. "Of course not. Why would you think that?"

She shrugged. "It's not even so much that I think that. I guess I was just wondering that."

"We're not a sexist community." Terk smiled broadly. "And these energy abilities are hard to find in anyone, … male or female. So, if this is something you want to develop and to train on, we can talk. It does come down to what your level of commitment will be."

"I get it," Mariana said. "At least I'm trying to get it. What I understand to a certain extent is that I have a connection with some of the team." She looked at Terk to see if she should continue or not.

He nodded.

"Like my connection with Terk, for example," Mariana

pointed out. "I don't think everyone knows about that."

"When you mentioned something about communicating with Terk earlier, we wondered," Tasha replied immediately. "So that's how you communicated with her on Cal's condition?" she asked Terk directly.

"To a certain extent. Sometimes I used the phone but not always. As it turns out, she is one of the easiest telepaths I've ever worked with," he noted.

Tasha and Sophia and Lorelei just gazed from one to the other.

"Wow," Tasha said, getting her voice first. "Mariana definitely needs to be working with us then."

"Not so fast," Terk replied, with a gentle smile. "She has to *want* to work with us. And she has to understand the danger."

"I think I've got that part down," Mariana teased, with a half-laughing groan.

"You do and you don't." Terk studied her for a long moment.

"I didn't realize you were doing so many missions," Mariana admitted.

"Calum can communicate with people a great distance away. But again, he's not back up to snuff, so his abilities are currently pretty limited in comparison to what he used to do."

"And those are the kind of abilities we're talking about, right?" Mariana asked. "Because he's never told me."

"That's because he's not free to speak of it," Terk explained. "I hate to be so businesslike or controlling, but NDAs are in place for a reason."

She stared at him and then snorted. "You're right. I hadn't even considered something so simple."

"It's far more complicated than that," Terk replied, "just because it's government work."

"Right, but it's not anymore, is it?"

"Correct. At the moment, it is not."

"So it's settled then," Mariana stated. "This is something we should be discussing. Maybe we need to set up something on a business level, that would cover everybody and allow us to keep functioning as we are going forward."

Terk now looked at her anew and asked, "You have several businesses, don't you?"

"Yes. I run them from home. Why do you ask?"

"How did you set them up?"

She smiled. "I started with my brother, an attorney— although, once you know some key details, it's not all that difficult to replicate as needed."

"We could use some help setting up an optimal business front for us," Terk noted.

"I can do that," Mariana replied, "at least a lot of it. And, if we do need a lawyer to review the documents I'll create, well, that's what my brother does."

"Maybe we'll take a look at that at some point." Terk smiled at her, noting how quickly her whole demeanor had changed. "We'll need to get this current mess sorted out first, of course."

"Definitely. Let's get Sean Calvert sorted out right now," Mariana stated. "Once we get everybody safely back home and healthy again, maybe we can all discuss it."

"But it won't stay calm for long," Terk reminded her. "The attack on the team was much larger than one man with a grudge against Calum. We won't be done with this until we get to the very bottom of the larger picture and understand who and what is behind the attack on the whole team."

She nodded. "I understand. Not to worry. I'm not over-simplifying."

"Good." Terk nodded. "As far as forming a new team goes, everybody would love to see something happen afterward, but we must be completely autonomous and separate from the government. Nothing like broken trust to change your thinking."

"Isn't that the truth." Her spirits vastly improved. Mariana walked over and refilled her coffee cup. Then suddenly she froze, the cup in her hand. "I get the idea that he thinks he knows what's happening—but he really doesn't."

"Can you expand on that?" Terk asked calmly.

She stared at him but realized that he was looking for any intel that she had to offer. "All I can tell you is that they see only the one person. But somebody else is there. I feel like it's up high though. I can't see him. I can only sense him."

"Terk, can you tell Calum that?" Tasha asked, busily typing, while checking the computer screens.

"Mariana needs to relay the message," Terk replied. "I think that would be the most helpful right now."

Mariana nodded. She closed her eyes and contacted Calum, then immediately passed over the message. "I've delivered it," she stated, "but I'm not sure he has received it, if that makes any sense."

Terk let out an odd laugh. "It makes more sense than you understand right now. I'll send the same message, so, between us, we ensure he gets it."

CAL SKIRTED ALONGSIDE the house. Everything in his head

was a little on the wonky side—getting crowded in there. He sent out mental messages to get everyone to just shut up. He wasn't sure if this added clutter were the other members of his team or someone else entirely, but Cal was struggling to sort out the clamoring in his head.

Not only just sort out but to even make sense of. He didn't understand why, all of a sudden, he heard this cacophony of sounds. It wasn't the same as if they had put up one of their noise barriers and had it running again. This was something completely different, and he didn't understand it.

He didn't like it one bit either.

Trying to clear his head so he could make sense of his surroundings was imperative. He sent a message to Terk, asking him to butt out if it was him. When Cal got no response, he assumed Terk had gotten the message and had listened. That would be something at least.

When a response came shortly, it was more of an impression instead of words. Something about a shooter up high. Immediately he searched the area around him.

A sniper. That wasn't something he'd expected from these guys, but he should have. *Damn it.* Or maybe not.

Nothing was quite the way he had expected it to be. As he slipped forward, he worried he'd missed something else. Those things you didn't know about were what always caught you up. He couldn't blame anyone but himself in this case.

He charged ahead, knowing they needed to capture Sean, preferably alive, so they could talk some sense into him. Cal had no wish to take away Tay's last remaining family member, but the reality was that Sean's survival was unlikely at best, especially if he wouldn't come in peacefully.

Sometimes Cal just hated his job. The fact that this person, who used to be a friend, had gone after his family was completely inexcusable. Cal understood from the point of view of the enemy that it was inevitable, but it wasn't that way from Cal's perspective. He would do anything to protect his son. Even though he hadn't spent that much time with him in an effort to protect him, the bond he felt to the child was amazing. He understood now Terk's whole issue over Celia and their unborn child.

Keeping their families safe was just a nightmare waiting to happen, and Cal hoped they could find a solution for it. But he also knew that, at this point in time, everybody was on board to protect his family. He knew they were. It was just one of those scenarios where there was no good answer. And they needed a good answer. Hell, at this moment, any kind of halfway decent answer that would get them out of this nightmare would do.

Surely Mariana and Little Calum didn't deserve to be tormented, caught in the struggle of good versus evil in the world. Cal had sacrificed having them in his life to protect them; yet they still were targeted. He had missed all that time with them, and for what? Shaking his head to refocus his attention, he then peered around the corner to see what was going on, almost instantly pulling back. But not fast enough. He had been seen. A shot had been fired. He heard a *ping*, and a chunk of concrete flew off the corner in front of him.

"Well, that answered that question," he muttered to himself. Obviously they were gunning for him and knew that he—and Damon—were here. Not exactly what Cal would have considered the best option. But still, he was here, and he would do what he could to find his way to Sean.

And capturing Sean was paramount.

That man couldn't continue on this path.

Ducking down low, Cal peered around the same corner again, looking for his next spot to move to. When the concrete in front of him was once again chipped off by a bullet, he swore to himself, realizing he was more or less pinned in place, yet had to find a way to get out. He needed to get away from here, but the shooter had him boxed in.

When a man called out, there was laughter behind his words. "And here you thought *you* were the best of the best."

He winced, frustrated that he was in this position with Sean. That was definitely a military motto.

"*I* am the best," Sean called out from a distance. "And this time you'll know it."

Calum didn't say anything; he just studied his surroundings, looking for a way out. Either find a way out or get higher. That was possible, just not the best answer because he'd probably take a bullet in the process, and that wouldn't help down the road.

He needed to have his full physical capacity in order to take down this asshole alone. Not that Sean was that good, but he was fueled with a long-burning anger, and that made him dangerous.

Cal studied the layout around him and noted a tree that was almost attainable. He poked his head around the corner a third time, and, as the concrete burst in front of him yet again, he flew toward his chosen spot. The bullets were still flying, but he made it. At that point in time, he realized that, although this sniper might be prepared, he wasn't as skilled as he needed to be for this job.

That was the good news.

The bad news was that the sniper was still good enough,

and, if Calum got sloppy, it was Game Over. What his team couldn't handle right now was to have anything else go wrong.

Sean laughed. "I just let you off on that one."

Of course he hadn't, but that was his way of dealing with failure. He'd always been quick to joke and to laugh, mocking a system if he felt it wasn't fair to him, such as the military.

"What's the matter?" Sean asked. "Are you scared to let me know you're here?"

"You're the one who should be scared," Cal called back.

"Oh, no. I've been waiting for this."

"Well, I'm here," Calum called back. "No need to wait for any longer."

"Yeah, but, you know, I don't want it to be over too soon."

"I'm sure your sister would appreciate that." Calum tried to distract Sean by poking at his emotions by bringing up his sister.

"You had no right to break up with her! She's the one who breaks up with people. She is gold, and you are nothing but a piece of shit."

He wondered at that kind of mentality that saw everybody in their best light, as long as they were on good terms with Sean. Cal didn't have anything to say about that, knowing perfectly well what had really happened with Tay.

The fact that Sean didn't know really sucked, since the truth would be a rude awakening for him. Especially considering the fact that he'd carried this grudge for years, all based on a lie. But Calum wasn't into giving him a truth bomb right now. The task at hand was to get the hell out of here in one piece, taking Sean down in the process.

"You won't get me, you know?" Sean taunted in a mocking conversational tone.

"I can see you almost trying to figure it out, thinking how to pull me into your web of lies and to make this into some sort of blazing triumph for you," Cal replied, "but you are doomed to fail." Calum was trying to get to him.

"This has nothing to do with your success. This is all about mine. And I have been a success, you know," he stated in that braggart tone again. "I've made something out of my life." Sean was adamant.

"Obviously not," Calum called back. "Otherwise you wouldn't be living with Tay. You wouldn't still be stuck on revenge for something that I had nothing to do with." There came an obvious moment of shock by Sean.

"What do you mean, you had nothing to do with anything?" he snapped. "You think I didn't see that you got me kicked out of the BUD/s training?" His voice was loud and angry now.

At that, Calum swore. "Do you really think that is something any of the recruits can do?" he asked.

"You went to the CO, and you told him that I was unstable."

Cal hadn't, but, considering what he was going through at this moment, it would have obviously been the right call if he had. "I didn't," he called back. "Not sure where you got the idea that I did, but it's not true."

"I saw you," Sean yelled. "You were talking to him!"

"Of course I was talking to him. I had to talk to him all the time, same as you, … and everybody else," Cal noted, realizing his former friend had more than a few blind spots over the issues between them.

"I knew exactly what you were doing."

"No, Sean. You're lying to yourself because you wanted it to be true, so you'd have something to blame for your shortcomings. I had nothing to do with you being kicked out," Cal said. "That's all on you. You failed the testing requirements."

"You know you're not getting out of this alive," he yelled, followed by a bark of laughter.

Calum looked around. "You and how many others, Sean?" Cal replied. "Because you know you can't do this on your own. Some things just take more skill than you've got." Cal knew that would get to Sean. What he wasn't expecting was the immediate and random pepper spray of gunfire all around him.

It revealed a lot about Sean's mental state and how dangerous he would be if Cal pursued this avenue of pissing off Sean. As tempting and potentially entertaining as it may be to do so, clearly it would just not be productive. Not in the current situation. "What if I just want to talk to you?" Cal asked.

"What will you do, whine about your wife and your kid?"

"Interesting that you chose somebody I'm not even with anymore." At that, another moment of shocked silence came.

"That's BS," he snapped. "My intel was good."

Cal shrugged. "You may have gotten intel, but it wasn't current." Again, more gunfire came his way. From his position, he saw where the gunfire was coming from, and it looked like Sean was on the upper deck of the neighbor's house. Cal had to distract Sean while also giving Damon a heads-up. "Do the neighbors know you're using their house?"

"I don't think he'll give a shit."

"What? Did you kill him too?" Cal asked in a conversational tone. "I suppose you killed your brother as well, *huh?* Then told your sister it was me?" Yet another moment of shocked silence came.

"I didn't fucking kill my brother," he growled in the low mean tone of voice.

"You know you did, but, hey, that's your pattern. I guess it's much easier for you to blame me than to take responsibility for your own issues."

"If it wasn't you," Sean asked, "who was it?"

"Well, if it wasn't me and if it wasn't you," Calum replied, "then you know perfectly well who it was. The same guys who have been cleaning up all along, using you as a pawn to do their dirty work. They tend to keep themselves out of the mess they hire the locals to do. However, after that, they do a pretty thorough job of cleaning up behind them."

"Well, you have made a few enemies," Sean jeered, with a laugh.

"It used to be a case of you could judge a man by his enemies," Cal told him.

"Ha. … Right now, it's you who seems to have the problem, Cal. You just piss off everybody."

That was an odd comment to make, and one Cal would have to ponder later. "If you say so," Calum told the empty space between them. Cal saw where Sean was, and Cal knew that Damon had to be out there, trying to come up and around on the side, to get a hold of Sean. That didn't mean he'd be successful though. Sean was a bit of an asshole at the best of times, but he obviously couldn't resist a good conversation about what he would do next, and that would be his downfall.

Cal heard more voices in the background of his mind again, and he wished to God they would shut up. He mentally dampened all the noise in the back of his head. He needed a clear head for this and didn't need the rest of his team chiming in. If there was something going on and they were trying to let him know, that was a different story. Yet, even as Cal looked around, he couldn't see anything. He figured one person was in Tay's house and another one here as a backup for Sean. Where Tay was by now, he didn't know. "You'll get your sister killed with this get-rich scheme of yours. You know that, right?"

"If you touched a hair on her head," he yelled in a hard voice.

"I haven't touched her," Cal said cheerfully. "*Yet.* But aren't you kind of an eye-for-an-eye guy?" At that, Sean started swearing again. "You do realize that, being as unhinged as you are, these guys won't keep you around, right?"

"Who and what are you talking about?"

"The guys who hired you," Cal said. "The ones who have the lovely little IT gig going on and wanted to hire your brother. Too bad you showed David all that mess. He would probably still be alive if you hadn't."

"Well, of course I had to show him. How else would he know what work needed to be done?"

"See? That just signed his death warrant," Cal noted quietly. "You never did get that whole confidentially thing, did you?"

There was a moment of silence. "They had no reason to kill my brother," he said, not as loudly as he had been talking.

But Calum heard a note of uncertainty, and he would

take advantage of it. "I hope you're right," he murmured, "because I'd hate to think that you could be guilty of that too."

"What do you mean *that too*?" he asked. "I'm not guilty of anything."

"Oh, so you're not the one who kidnapped Mariana?"

"I should just kill the bitch and your son anyway."

Calum's blood boiled at the comment. "I'm sure you may put that on your to-do list, but I'm here to tell you it ain't happening."

"What will you do about it?" he asked, laughing.

"Well, you won't be surviving the day," Cal noted. "If not me killing your sorry ass, it'll be the guys you're working for."

"Nope, no way," he argued. "I'm far too useful to them."

"Yeah, yeah, yeah …" Cal said, his tone weary. "We've heard that story before. I think David is body number sixteen that we've found so far, including five who were IT types." He heard Sean suck in his breath at that.

"What kind of IT?"

"Well, two developed some ear implant software that kills the wearer. Two more were working on the drones that they're using. One invented software for it. But, of course, he's done and gone now. Too bad, he was just a kid. And the fifth one was your brother."

"You're lying." Again, with a note of uncertainty.

"I don't have any reason to lie," Cal said quickly. "You're far too deep into something that's way over your head. And Tay will die too, just by association with you. So it won't end anywhere close to the way that you were hoping it would."

"You don't know anything about it," Sean snapped.

"No, I don't know your situation, but I've seen it time and time again. That's the thing about the work we do. And I've got an awful lot of years of experience," Cal noted. "Years of seeing shit go down that nobody ever hears about. And you can't do anything about that. Shit happens, Sean."

"Of course it does," he said, with a sneer. "It just depends on which side of it you happen to be on."

"Meaning, you're hoping that you're on the right side? Well, let me tell you. You're on the wrong side, just like your brother was. If you're lucky, you might save your sister," he added, "but, if she's involved in this or if you've told her things, she's already done and gone."

"She's not involved in anything," he snapped. "I told her that I was thinking about setting you up, and she thought it was a hell of an idea."

"Of course she did because, just like you, she hasn't got any sense of self. She hasn't got any real awareness of how life operates or what happens when you get yourself into shit like that because now she's an accessory."

"It doesn't matter. If we don't get caught, she's not an accessory to anything."

Cal just shook his head at the naïve blindness. "It's not that easy, man."

"You don't even have any government affiliations anymore. They told me everything."

"Did they now? Sorry to tell you, but they lied."

"Nope, they didn't. Now you're the one who's lying." He laughed like a lunatic.

"What makes you think I'm lying?" he asked.

"The fact that three-quarters of your team is down."

"How is it that you even knew I was up again?" he asked his old acquaintance. Some things just started to filter through the air, and Cal had no idea what that was. He figured, if there was any way to find out more about the kidnapping, he should try. "How did you find her?" he asked, puzzled.

"Social media." He laughed again. "It seems my beautiful sister was browsing for Calums and found your son. Of course we weren't sure if he was related or not at first, but it didn't take very long to put two and two together."

Cal stared out in the distance. "Bloody social media." It was something he hated himself and had no idea that Mariana would have gone there, but, yeah, why wouldn't she? She didn't know the dangers. "Well, I'm sorry to say that you found her, but she's also safe right now."

"I found her once. I'll find her again," he swore, with such a dismissive attitude that Calum felt the fury boiling again.

"Why don't you come down here, and we can talk, man-to-man."

"Oh no," Sean said, "I know how that works. I come down there, and you start firing."

"Nope. Not at all," he stated. "But are you really planning on taking your sister down with you for this?"

"She's not going down. I already talked to the bosses, and they told me that we were in the clear."

"Jesus …" The stupidity of this man just blew Cal away. He closed his eyes and sent out a probe. If he could at least do the shake-the-tail thing that Gage could do, then Sean would have a freak-out and give those guys of his something to consider at least. But first Cal needed to disrupt that calm certainty in Sean's world somehow.

The trouble was, Cal didn't exactly have the same skill set that Gage did. They all had different abilities, with a variety of strengths and weaknesses. But he reached out mentally, searching for and finding the energy in the house across from him, in the small Juliet balcony off the master bedroom. Sean just stood there, with what looked like an AK-47 in his hand. "Nice gun," he said softly.

But, of course, Sean couldn't hear him. *Or could he?* He got closer and closer and, with a probe of energy, sent his voice along that energy trail and whispered, "Nice gun, Sean."

Cal watched, as immediately Sean jumped and spun around, his gun up, yelling, "Who was that? Where are you? Show yourself!" He started firing randomly. Obviously either nobody was home and around for the day or this was a completely deserted neighborhood area because surely, with all this gunfire, somebody would have called the cops by now. "You're not worried about your neighbors calling the cops on you?" Cal called out.

"I don't give a shit," Sean yelled. "Most of them don't even live here anyway. Besides, once I'm out of here, it won't matter. And, hey, if the cops show up, and I'm still here, maybe I'll just take them out too."

With the casualness of his tongue, Cal realized that Sean really had crossed a point of no return. "So you'll just kill a cop because he shows up for the call of duty?"

"Why the hell not?"

"What happened to the man all about honor and re-spect?"

"Yeah, well, … *that* man," Sean explained, "got kicked out of where he planned on spending his life because of somebody he always knew was an asshole."

"I didn't do it, Sean. I get that you won't take responsi-bility for your failings, so you've glommed on to a reason that you're hoping is viable, but it just isn't true. I didn't do it."

"You know what, Cal? It doesn't matter if you did or you didn't."

Cal worried about the sudden weariness in Sean's tone that made Calum worry that this could become a suicide-by-cop scenario.

"If you're right, I'm a dead man. If you're wrong, I'll get the hell out of here and find a place to live where I can get some peace back in my world."

"I want that for you too," Cal replied.

"Bullshit. You don't care. You just want me to get the hell out of your life and to leave your family alone."

"What would you want if it were your family?"

"I would already have killed the guy." Then he laughed and laughed. "But that's just me."

"That's too bad, Sean, because I know what you don't—that these guys are cold-blooded and damn dangerous." More gunfire came Cal's way, and he realized Sean had taken that as an insult.

"You think you're so much better than me, don't you? You always have. So you think I'm nothing but chopped liver, and I'll just let these guys walk all over me?" he asked. "What you forget is that they *need* me," Sean snapped, "and I'm just like them. I belong."

It was hard to imagine why anybody would want to be just like these guys, but his old friend was so far gone into his own private world that he couldn't see the obvious reality in front of him.

"I'm sorry," Cal called out. "Apparently we'll just agree to disagree on that one."

"Yeah, you think?" he snapped. "Well, I think you're

nothing but a lying son of a bitch, and I'm done playing."

Sean stepped farther out on the balcony, Calum saw him through the trees and realized that whatever was coming down would be a whole lot more serious.

Sean peppered the entire vegetation Cal had used to screen his presence, the bullets flying everywhere. He slipped farther down, knowing that he wasn't anywhere close to being out of range.

Just then he saw Damon reach the balcony. And, when the guns went off this time, it was a completely different type of weapon.

CHAPTER 6

MARIANA HUDDLED IN her chair, staring at Terk. "They're talking," she murmured.

He nodded, his gaze boring into hers. "I can hear that. Can you make out any of the words?"

She frowned. "They're shouting insults at each other," she noted, with a caustic tone, "or at least Sean's insulting Cal."

Terk's lips twitched. "You sound surprised."

She shook her head. "I shouldn't be, should I?"

"Nope," he agreed quietly. "It's fairly typical."

"I guess," she muttered, as she closed her eyes, wishing that this would all just go away. "These gifts don't make it any easier, do they?"

"No, of course not," he replied. "You're in a position to hear some of what's going on, yet not able to do anything about it. You can see some of what's going on around him but not the whole picture."

She opened her eyes again to see that the other women had gathered closer. "I'm sorry. I'm not trying to be difficult. I'm not used to sharing what I overhear."

"You're doing fine. This isn't an easy thing," Tasha exclaimed. "I've worked with Terk for years, and I saw several of the men brought on board and understood what they were going through as he taught them. But honestly, you're the first female."

"At the same time, we didn't expect to have any abilities either. So what is bringing it on?" Mariana exclaimed, looking over at Terk.

"Well, you said you had some experiences before."

"Sure, but nothing like this," she murmured. "And it's not like I had much of a relationship with Cal before."

Terk gave her a droll look.

She flushed. "Okay, fine, but he didn't want me around."

"He didn't want you around to keep you safe," he corrected.

She raised both hands in mock surrender. "Whatever. I'm not suspecting his motives, just his methodology."

At that, Tasha burst out laughing. "Oh my gosh, that's good. You keep believing that."

Mariana glared at her. "Am I being a fool?" she asked. "Am I—"

"No," Tasha interrupted. "But the relationships we have all found are extremely intense and bonded in a way. As in fated."

Raising an eyebrow, Mariana asked, "Well, if that's the case, why was Cal wasting so much damn time?"

"I had the same problem," Tasha shared. "Damon avoided me and everything to do with me because he didn't want to get involved with someone at work and didn't want me to get hurt from the association either. So, as soon as this was all being shut down, we were both privately making plans to see whether something was there between us or not. Although it didn't get that far, I was planning on talking to him, and he was planning on talking to me, but we never did, ... until after the attack."

"Right." Mariana nodded. "I did get a message from Calum—before the accident—saying that he wanted to see me."

"Well, that's good, right?"

"Except, for all I know," she replied, "he just wanted to see his son. He had visited Little Calum occasionally before." She added, "And he knew about him from the first, if anybody wonders. I didn't hide it."

"Good, but I'm sure he wanted to come see both of you," Tasha added.

Mariana frowned at that. "Still, it feels weird. Like I'm here by default or something."

"Well, you did finagle your way into being here," Tasha pointed out, not letting her get away with thinking anything else.

Mariana flushed. "Was I wrong?" she asked in a low voice. "It didn't feel safe anywhere else."

"That's because you *are* safe here," Tasha murmured. "We'll make arrangements to take over more of the building."

She looked over at Terk. "Any progress with those arrangements yet?"

"Ice is working on it," he murmured.

"Oh, good," Mariana replied. "Maybe they can rent different parts of it under different companies, just to keep everybody guessing."

"I think that's the plan—or some version of that." Terk shrugged.

Mariana shook her head. "It's hard to believe, knowing one attack already took the team out—or at least down."

"You're not wrong there," Terk bit off. "But that doesn't mean it'll happen a second time. As far as we understood at the time, we were out of business."

She nodded. "And, therefore, you weren't expecting an attack."

"No," he stated.

"And that's why you're thinking it's governmental?"

"I'm not sure how much of it is our government. This all may have started with them. But, as it unfolds, I've come to believe it then became kind of a wild card mission for any number of people who had grudges against us."

"Ah." Mariana nodded. "I can see that too. You appear to have the ability to read into situations," she noted, with half a smile.

He nodded absentmindedly. "We aren't sure that's a bad thing though."

"Well, I guess it depends on why you're pissing them off," she replied. "I can't say I like knowing that you and your team will always be a target."

"That's not necessarily so," Terk argued. "If we go private and stay fairly close to the ground, most people won't know anything about us."

"So why is it a problem now?"

"Because they took out so many of us," he explained. "Energy is spread pretty thin right now, and I can do only so much on my own. That is why I brought in and trained the team to begin with."

"So are you saying that, if your team was up and functioning, you would do a lot more?"

He nodded. "A *lot* more," he repeated, for emphasis. "Including tracking all these people in ways that they have no idea of. We can also do a lot more remote viewing, which is Calum's specialty, but he doesn't appear to be back up to that level of recovery yet."

"*Remote viewing*," Mariana repeated, rolling the phrase around in her head. "So how does that even work? I'm a little scared to ask, but I presume that means he could be sitting here with us, yet looking at something in another part of the world?"

"Exactly," Terk confirmed.

"And, if we ever got everybody's shit back together again, we could set up a private company—to continue doing what you did for the government? Is that what you would want?"

He hesitated and then shrugged. "I don't know what I want," Terk admitted. "I just know that I want to solve this and to ensure that none of us have a target on our backs like that anymore."

At that, Tasha stepped in. "And really it would be a hell of a lot better if we could set up privately," she added. "One of the hardest things is the fact that we've always had to play by the government's rules. Without them, we could set up a much higher level of security and take on jobs that we choose to do. Like Ice and Levi, right?"

"Something like that, yes," Terk agreed. "Maybe with an even higher level of energy to keep things safe."

"How many people know how many of you are working on this team now?" Mariana asked, bewildered. "Surely there can't be too many who know of your team."

"No, only if they came across us on a mission," he murmured. "Which is also why Iran is of particular interest."

Mariana nodded slowly. "I get that you think Iran is of particular interest, but what if they don't think so?"

He turned and looked at her. "What do you mean?"

"Well, what if Iran is just watching you. Now that you're surfacing a little bit more, and they realize not everybody is dead, they'll be wondering what the real story is." Mariana was deeply lost in her own thoughts. "Anybody who sees you now as weaker can take advantage of that fact and can jump in at some point, unless they are sitting back to wait and see if someone else will do it first."

"Do you think somebody else is involved?" he asked.

"I don't know anything, Terk," Mariana admitted, holding up her hands. "All I can say is, to the rest of the world, you're a mess—whether dying, recovering, disbanded—without support."

Everybody nodded. She was right about that.

"I'm sure most of them are probably trying to figure out if they can take you out permanently."

"That occurred to me, yes," Terk agreed, with a clipped nod. "We are trying to track as many different factions as we can."

At the same time, a computer beeped. Tasha hopped up and said, "And that could be one of them right there." She walked over, sat down, and clicked on the keys. "Definitely movement out of Iran right now," she confirmed. "Remember the site that was bombed on our Iran mission? Apparently another building fairly close to it has some activity." She brought it up on video. "Here." She pointed to a desolated area. "This is where the demolition happened and where that group was taken out. But here"—she pointed over just a few hundred meters—"look at this building." They watched as somebody opened the door, stepped out, and looked around, then went back inside again. A few minutes later he stepped out with somebody who needed help to walk.

Terk leaned forward. "Can you get a close-up on his face?"

Tasha immediately started working the keys.

"Well, I'll be damned. That's Lui Pul, one of Yousef's men, one of the Iranian team that we attacked," Terk noted. "We weren't sure if anybody survived."

"As far as we knew," Tasha murmured beside him, "we were pretty sure nobody had."

"Well, we were wrong," Terk noted. "That's Lui Pul."

She nodded. "Maybe, but why doesn't that name sound Iranian?"

"Fake European name," Terk replied.

Tasha nodded, her voice heavy. "Keep talking, and I'll keep tracking this."

"Also track any of Yousef's kin. He had a brother, Zaid. See if you can find him. I figure he went dark, so keep at it."

Tasha nodded. "Got it."

"Could you fill in those of us who don't know the details here?" Lorelei asked from the table.

At that, Mariana turned. "The problem is," she murmured, "I have these feelings and know things, but I don't know what it is."

"It's a special gift," Terk explained simply. "It's a connection with somebody on a level that most people can never ever hope to achieve."

Tasha and Sophia nodded.

"I would agree with that," Mariana said.

Lorelei piped up. "Well, I have no idea what it is, but I'm not against using it to show Gage that we belong together."

At that, Tasha laughed. "Hear, hear! Life has already pushed us to the brink in so many ways that, as far as I'm concerned, it also means that life is too short and that we need to do whatever we can to enjoy the time we have," she murmured. "If nothing else that's what this has brought home for me."

Terk looked at her, with a knowing smile.

She asked him, "You knew how I felt?"

He nodded. "I did, indeed. And I think you're right. I think this is all a lesson about living the type of life that we want to live," he murmured. "And, although there could be adaptations or challenges ahead, if it's what you want, then it's what you need to reach out and to grab hold of."

"*Hmm*, I wonder if that would work in my case," Mariana said, with a laugh.

Terk smiled, as he looked over at her. "You are not far off from having everything you want in that relationship," he noted. "So just hold on tight, yet give him some leeway, and remember to let him go, so he can come back."

Mariana frowned.

Sophia then spoke up. "When you love—and you *truly*, truly love—it's important to let whoever you love go and to let them do whatever they need to do, and, if it's a true and abiding love, they'll find their way back to you."

Mariana sighed. "You know what? I love the sound of that but the waiting—"

The three other women all burst out laughing. "All of us have been there," Sophia added. "As a matter of fact, it's such an obvious trend or pattern in our lives that I'm surprised Terk hasn't brought it up."

"I'm still trying to figure out how to categorize it," he noted, with a hint of sarcasm. "It's not as if we've ever seen anything like this before."

"Very true," Lorelei murmured. "And maybe there's a reason for that. Maybe what we're seeing isn't so much new and different as it was a state of becoming."

"I think it was the accident," Terk added. "We needed the extra support around the team, as well as your added gifts."

"Maybe," Mariana replied, "maybe these gifts of ours were a result of the accident. Maybe we're just seeing the tip of the iceberg of all this."

"I don't know yet," Terk admitted, his tone quiet and contemplative. "If only I knew what that meant for Celia."

"On that matter, I have no idea," Mariana whispered.

Sophie walked over and placed a hand on his shoulder. "So far, nothing that we've found tracks back to her."

"No," Terk agreed. "In this case, Calum is the only one who seems to have a personal vendetta involved."

"And maybe," Tasha added, "that was just a complete coincidence." Terk looked over at her, and she winced. "Okay, I remember. There are no coincidences in this world."

"At least none," Lorelei clarified, "that we can really count on. It seems like something's always going on."

"Agreed," he murmured. Then he stood. "The men have to be trusted to do what they're doing. We'll monitor and give them all the aid and energy that we can, but we just have to let them do what they need to do."

"And if they do a crappy job?" Mariana asked, surprising them all.

Terk let out a half-hearted chuckle at that. "Well, we hope that's not the case, but, if that's what it is, then that's what it is."

She nodded. "So, in other words, don't help, don't do anything?"

"Honestly, I think we're hurting more than helping sometimes," Terk suggested. "Not with our intent but with our delivery. These guys have so much chatter going on in their heads that another voice added in can seriously deter and distract them. And we don't always know the whole picture of what they are dealing with at any given moment out there." Terk sighed.

"As I've told the guys many times before, we get glimpses and pieces and parts that we must put together in the right way." He looked around the room at the women gathered here. "I suspect we need a clearinghouse, so that one person delivers any messages you all have. Of course there will be exceptions. If it's a split second to notify someone of impending death, go for it."

"I agree with Terk on that," Tasha stated, "and it feels very much like the guys were shutting us down. Yet Damon could at least turn on the damn Bluetooth again, but it's hard to contact him."

"I'll send him a text." Terk pulled out his phone. He stopped, looking at his cell screen. "They've been there quite a while, haven't they?"

"They've been there a long time," Tasha murmured, her tone hardening.

"At what point in time is it too long?" Mariana asked.

"It's not too long yet. Missions like this can take hours. And, in this particular case, somebody is playing cat and mouse with a gun." Just then his phone rang. He looked down. "Well, speak of the devil. Calum?"

"Yeah, it's me. We didn't do it, but he's down."

"Who's down?"

"Calvert," he said, "Sean is down. And I don't think he'll make it."

"Shit," Terk replied. "We don't need any more bodies. Even Levi and Ice will have a hard time sorting these all out."

"He's definitely been involved with these guys after us, and who knows what other sketchy stuff Sean's been into. I'm sure we'll dig up a bunch of trouble, once we go looking," Damon replied, "but that's not the reason I'm calling. Damon had just come up behind Sean, as he was peppering the bushes all around me. Before Damon could capture him, somebody took him out with a single shot."

"Another sniper?" Terk asked sharply. "If Sean can even be counted as the first sniper ..."

"Sean was no sniper," Cal murmured, "so we have one we couldn't see."

"Damn it ..."

"And one more thing," Calum added, his voice harsh. "It also leaves Tay alone now."

"Is Sean dead?"

"Not yet, but I don't think he'll make it."

"Shit," Terk murmured. "And I suppose she has nothing new to add?"

"She didn't have much to add in the first place, but now I'm sure she'll blame me for this."

"It sounds like she was far more than an absentminded observer in this whole thing," Terk noted, "so you need to let go of that guilt trip."

"I hear you. The problem is, these brothers were her only family."

"Again, not your fault," Terk stated.

"Yeah, I know, but, at the same time, ... it just sucks. We'll take a look around. Sean would have had a partner—not the sniper—so we'll track him down. I'm thinking he's at Tay's house, so we're going there. After we see what we can find, we'll head back." With that, he hung up.

Terk looked back over at Lorelei and Tasha. "See if you

can tear apart Sean's life any further. He's about to become a statistic."

They both winced.

"I hear you there," Tasha noted, "but it really sucks that we never find any live witnesses."

"More than sucks," Terk replied. "It's one more link that these guys have taken out before we could."

"Which is why they've done it."

At that, he got up.

"But is Calum okay?" Mariana asked.

Terk nodded. "He's okay."

"Did he say he was okay?" she pushed.

He looked at her in surprise. "I didn't ask, but he didn't tell me any differently."

She frowned and nodded. "I don't know what, but something just feels wrong."

"Wrong in what way?" Terk asked.

Everybody in the room stopped and turned to face her.

She swallowed and raised her hands. "I don't do this stuff, so I can't tell you," she said in frustration. "Something just feels very wrong."

Terk repeated her words, as if pondering the meaning of them.

She shook her head. "I don't know. I don't know. How, what, why? None of it, ... so please don't ask. I just know that something is wrong."

"Like another shooter?"

Mariana frowned. "Maybe, or maybe the shooting isn't over. Maybe somebody else will kill Cal."

"Ah," Terk said, pulling out his phone. When there was no answer, he frowned and started spamming out texts.

"What are you doing?" she asked. "What are you saying?"

"Warning him, reminding Cal that the sister is still there and may not be as innocent as she may have led everyone to believe."

"She's not innocent at all," Mariana stated, with another hard-hitting insight. "She was way more involved than Cal suspects."

Terk looked at her sharply and hit Dial on his phone. When he got no answer, he swore and changed to a different number.

"Can't you reach him in *other* ways?" Mariana asked.

"Yes, but I can't make things very clear to him in *other* ways." At that, somebody answered Terk's call, and he turned away to speak. "Damon, it's Terk. There is a good chance that the sister isn't as innocent as she appears. Just watch your back." He put it on Speakerphone, just in time for them all to hear Damon's voice.

"We've already got two bogeys," he noted, "and we're taking heavy fire."

"Do you want backup?"

"Yeah? Who'll do that?" he asked, with half a laugh.

"I know. We'll figure it out and get back to you as soon as we can." And, with that, he hung up, then turned and looked at the rest of them.

Immediately Tasha nodded. "Go ahead. This is a team effort, and they need you."

"You know that every one of those guys will be unhappy if I leave here right now."

"Well, every one of us will be unhappy," Sophia added, "if one of them gets hurt." He just glared at her, and she glared right back. "We've got this, Terk," Sophia stated. "And we'll try not to be insulted."

"Fine," Terk agreed. "By the time I get there, it may very well be over anyway." And, with that, he left immediately. As soon as he was gone, the four women looked at each other.

"Any update from Gage?" Tasha asked.

"No, they were checking out a different avenue and clearing some different addresses we had to check out," Sophia replied.

"Why don't we try to contact them and let them know what's going on?"

"On it already. I'm just not sure how far out of position they are," Sophia noted, already firing off messages.

Tasha looked over at Mariana. "Hey, don't look so worried," Tasha said. "Remember. These guys are professionals."

"They're good. I know," Mariana stated quietly. "But these are traps set by people who hate them—only because Terk's team has done so much to put them out of business. And rightly so of course."

Tasha immediately nodded. "Yes, we're talking about people who use innocent women and children to carry bombs into parking lots, to burn alive complete families because they didn't want to have anything to do with their plans."

At that, Mariana winced. "Right, terrorists of the worst kind."

"Exactly. Our guys have been dealing with it for a long time, and so have I, ... to a certain degree," Tasha added, "but the shock of it all never fails to rekindle the horror."

"How do you do this work day after day without burning out or going insane?" Mariana murmured.

"Like I told you before, once you understand what the danger is, you realize it could be you or somebody else you love. It could be anybody in your world at any time—which starts to bring home the reality that you need to do whatever you can to stop them."

"I get it," Mariana replied. "I really do, and I'm not trying to be naïve and innocent about it all. I just don't know how one is supposed to park all the fears and function in these conditions. Or maybe it's not a matter of parking the fears, as much as doing what needs to be done in spite of the fears," she noted.

"Listen," Tasha began. "There's no way to let any of this go, and it certainly won't just go away. The reality is, there will be no *us* if we don't work this case to the end. And, if you hope to have any kind of a life with Cal after this," she explained, "you must find a way to make peace with the work he does, that we all do."

"But how?" Mariana asked. "You heard Terk. Despite everything this team has gone through, they're talking about keeping this team together," she said, staring at Tasha. "How does that work? How will it be a different way, a better way?"

"Because, in that next scenario, we can control the circumstances of our surroundings and the cases," she told her. "You also have to understand that this is what these guys do. It is literally who they are. I don't know if they could stop doing this, even if they wanted to. We might all have it in our heads that retiring would be an ideal thing, but I'm not sure it would be good for them at all."

And that gave Mariana something to think about that she had yet to consider.

Maybe it wasn't fair to Calum to pull him away from all this. She wasn't sure that's even what she wanted to do, but it just seemed like everything out here was a problem. These were huge problems that they couldn't be expected to fix, not on such short notice. And maybe they weren't. Maybe they were only expected to fix the bits that they could. And that's probably what she was struggling with—that whole concept of doing it slowly, of figuring out what they could fix and what they couldn't. It just all seemed so ... overwhelming.

She sat here, as the chaos reigned around her. Communications were forged, and then suddenly it all went quiet. "What happens now?" she asked, with a sigh.

"Now we'll watch what we can on the satellite and wait." Tasha tapped the screen beside her.

With a surprised exclamation, Mariana hopped up and walked over to Tasha. "Seriously, is that what I think it is?"

"Yes, absolutely," Tasha confirmed. "We'll watch them handle their business and do what they have to do."

CAL STOOD IN the neighbor's bedroom and stared at Sean out on the balcony. He no longer breathed, so was officially dead now. Cal looked over at Damon. "You didn't see anyone else?"

"Nope." He pointed to where he figured the sniper had fired from. "He is just waiting. Probably for us to get to Sean or for whatever else this sniper wanted to do. Maybe give him a shot at us."

"I don't think he gave a shit about anything but Sean's kill shot, so the sniper had to sit and watch until then. I think he just waited for the best time to take out Sean with a single pull of the trigger."

"At any time," Damon asked Calum, "did he go after you at all?"

"No, I don't think so. Granted, Sean, in all his fury, was

spraying me with bullets a time or two. I think the sniper fired a single shot at Sean, and then he bolted."

"So, in other words, he took out his assigned target."

Cal nodded. "The sniper may well be gone. We might not have to worry about another shooter."

"Probably so, but better be safe than sorry," Damon noted.

"Yeah, I understand that. Things are getting a little hairy around here."

"More than a little," Damon said in disgust. "We really have to get ahead of these guys. Terk said something, and I'm not sure whether it's quite what he meant. I'm just wondering how much of this is personal and how much of it has nothing to do with us."

Cal looked at his buddy and stated, "You'll need to explain that a whole lot more."

Damon groaned. "I can't really do that because I'm a little confused myself. This is the first time in any of these attacks that we clearly found a personal element."

"I disagree," Cal argued, shaking his head. "Just because we didn't find a *team-related Sean* character to prove such a personal connection to our team doesn't mean someone taking us all down at once wasn't personal. Remember the initial attack? It was specifically engineered for those rare people, like us, with our unique skills. So, hell yes, sounds to me like all of this is damn personal."

"What are the chances that they were just utilizing Sean as the means to an end? And did they hire others, like Sean, who had personal vendettas against us, making this more personal?"

"I'm not exactly sure I get what you mean." Cal frowned.

"Because I'm not explaining it well," Damon replied. "And that's my fault. It's all still a little bit scary in my head."

"Well, take a few minutes to think about it," Calum suggested. "And I'd love to hear more. Especially if there was anything personal in the attacks on the rest of you, particularly the women."

"Well, Lorelei is interesting," Damon explained. "She was hit by a car under suspicious circumstances, and there were multiple attempts to take her out, one even back at the base. And do you think it had something to do with her reaching out to Gage?"

"That's what I'm wondering. I want to know how these guys knew so much about us and our special skills, about our women—whom we were even hiding from other members on the team?"

"And how did these guys find out Lorelei was even with us at that point?"

"I think she was hacked," Cal stated carefully. "I get that I missed a lot, but I'm pretty sure things have been getting hacked all along."

"If that were the case, these guys should have a lot more information on us, rather than running with this petty *revenge game* scenario."

"I think they're still putting it all together, and a lot of holes are in their intel." Cal shrugged.

"They thought this game would be 100 percent done, once we all died in their initial attack," Damon suggested. "That may have been their best shot at killing us. Now they have poked the bear and don't know what to do. Kinda like Sean when rattled and him spraying you with bullets. That seems to be what these guys are doing now. Since we're still alive, they're scrambling to regroup and to figure out how to take us out now. At the same time, they're trying to figure out why we're still alive."

"I'll confess to doing a little of that myself, and I think it all comes down to Terk."

Damon immediately nodded. "I'm right there with you on that one."

"I know it sounds stupid, but I'm not exactly sure what went on with Terk," Calum admitted.

"Well, after watching how hard it was on Terk, trying to keep energy going to everybody, I'm pretty damn sure we wouldn't be alive today if it weren't for him."

"I totally agree with that," Cal replied, "but it's just not helpful right now."

"The question we have to answer is, what does anybody gain by taking us out? What does anybody gain by having people brought in to make it personal? Like in this case, Sean was just an extra for them. They probably targeted our friends, like Mariana, and our enemies, like Sean. A double-pronged approach, hoping one or the other would work."

Silence. Damon continued, "In Lorelei's case, when they found out she hadn't died from the hit-and-run, they tried again and accidentally took out a stranger who resembled her," he shared.

"So that was just a freak accident? A wrong time, wrong place kind of deal?"

"For that dead woman, sure, but for Lorelei, they kept trying, and I think she was targeted because she was Gage's friend."

Calum suddenly realized what Damon was getting at. "So, hang on a minute. You're thinking that Mariana was supposed to be taken out, but instead they used her as a bait to lure me out—like Lorelei was targeted to get to Gage?"

Damon and Cal were talking it out, as they had so often before. They were trying to make sense of everything they knew, and now the mist was lifting.

"Somewhere along the line," Damon murmured, "these guys have found access to the friends in our world—which isn't something I would have thought was possible."

"Exactly. So where did they get that personal information from?" At that question from Cal, the two men stared at each other.

"I don't know," Damon admitted, "but that's a really good point. We'll need to tug that line and see."

"We have to take a look at everybody then. Family, friends, acquaintances, and virtually anyone we have been in contact with. It's one hell of a witch hunt."

"We need to see if anybody else has been targeted. Or taken or threatened or whatever. In your case, you've got Sean, but you've also got his sister."

"And I still don't know that she's terribly innocent or just faking it," Cal murmured, as he stared at her house.

"According to Terk, she might not be innocent at all," Damon stated.

"At this point, she isn't fully compromised, having done everything that they wanted done, but I think she's probably in too deep to walk away now."

"Which means, she's done."

"Yeah, she's very well likely to be taken out." At that, Cal did one final sweep of the immediate area. "No energies out there. I think the sniper is gone."

They turned, left the body to be picked up by Merk, and headed back to Tay's house.

"I get no readings here either. You?" When Damon

shook his head, Cal knocked on the door and called out, "Tay, open the door." When no answer came, he pushed it open and called out, "Tay!" And still got no answer. He looked over at Damon, raised an eyebrow.

"She was here when we headed out the back, right?" Damon asked Cal.

"Yeah, but did she take off?"

"Maybe she just couldn't stand the thought of something happening to her brother."

"That is quite possible," Calum agreed. "They were always the closest of the three siblings, but she and Sean got closer just recently. Regardless she won't be easy to reason with. I can promise you that."

"It doesn't matter if they were close or not at this point. It's just a huge mess, any way you look at it."

Together, they headed into the house, moving cautiously.

"I'll go upstairs and check," Cal told Damon. With that, he raced up the stairs, calling out, "Tay, are you up here?" When he still got no answer, he felt a horrible sense of helplessness.

"Dear God, you didn't have to kill her too," he whispered. The trouble was, if she were involved, even if only involved a little bit, she would be collateral damage, and these guys would just finish her off. Cal raced back downstairs. "Her bedroom and the whole second floor is empty."

"Yeah, it's all empty down here too," Damon noted. "You think she left?"

"If she was smart, she would have," he replied. "Just think about it. Her brother is in deep trouble, and everybody might be expecting that she's a part of it, and yet she might not know very much of anything. And, with her other brother dead, she's got to finally know how serious this is."

"I think she knew it was serious the minute we showed up," Damon stated. "Up until then, it was anything but."

"It was just a game, like a theoretical exercise which she really didn't have any connection to, because it wasn't her doing anything. Or was just her brother joking about it."

"Now the joke is on her," he murmured.

"And these are not very nice people to joke about," Cal added. "So, it is what it is. Now the question is, will we stay here and see if we can track her down?"

"I need to wait for Merk, who is coming with somebody from MI6 to take care of Sean's body," Damon shared. "At this point in time, I'm surprised MI6 is even still dealing with Merk, since we're making so much extra work."

"Good thing MI6 has someone to deal with this. Otherwise it might be Merk and Terk having the argument."

"I don't think that ever happens. Those two are close."

"It's a damn good thing they are," he murmured. "We don't have too many friends in this world."

"Not to mention the fact that somebody is looking after us."

"I'm glad that Terk has a … friend now at least," Cal added, and then he shook his head.

"You know what? I would say Celia's a partner but *Jesus*. That woman didn't have any choice in the matter either."

"We don't have her story yet, right?" Cal asked.

"No. I heard there was talk about her waking up, but I haven't learned anything else since then. I'm not certain that we'll know much either," Damon added.

"I'm sure Terk would like for all the rest of this crap to just go away, so he could get stateside and figure some of it out with her."

"Is that even an option?" he asked quietly.

"I hope so, for his sake. He doesn't deserve this."

"Neither does she."

"No, I gotcha. This whole thing is just a shit show from start to finish."

"Well, let's make sure that we finish it. Right now we're running out of people to even go after."

"Not necessarily," Cal argued. "We've got somebody who hired Sean and somebody who was in the brother David's world, so there must have been some communication."

"Tasha and crew are tearing that apart right now," Damon confirmed.

"Good. A part of me would really just like to go back to headquarters and let my mind gel over this one."

"And how much of that is also wanting to go back and see your son?"

"A lot," he admitted. "It's such a very strange thing to have a child. And, even though he's four years old, I don't know him that well."

"And are you angry about that?"

"No, only with myself, since it was my doing. I was so worried about keeping them safe that I left them on their own, and they weren't safe anyway. I checked in occasionally and saw to their needs, but, in the end, I still failed at the most important thing—being a good husband and a good dad. It just makes me sick to think of what could have happened. I've always liked the idea of having a wife and child," he admitted, "but I couldn't get past the idea that my presence would put them at risk. Even worse, I didn't really give her a way to communicate with me either." Cal shook his head. "When I cut it off, I cut it off, and I guess this is the kind of penalty you pay."

"I don't think you have to pay a penalty though," Damon stated, "not for long."

"I'm also hoping this guilt I have won't be long-term," he replied, with a smile. "I'm just not sure where she's at with it by now. She's been through a lot, and it's my fault."

"And how do you feel about her?"

"The same as I always did," he said, with half a smile. "I left her behind to keep her safe, not to let her down."

"I get it," Damon stated. "It's the reason we all walked, but, at the same time, it looks like the other people in our lives all got into trouble anyway. And that's the argument Tasha's using against me right now." He eyed his buddy. "So Mariana wants to be with you at least."

"She does, but I don't think she truly understands any of this," he noted, with a wave to himself. "What'll happen when she finds out about my gifts? I bet she'll run for the hills and stay there, and I'll be lucky if I ever get to see my son."

"I wouldn't write her off just yet," Damon replied. "I think she's smarter and tougher than you've given her credit for."

"I hope so," he murmured, "because she needs to be. This won't be an easy walk. And even being with us will be a hard adjustment for her. She's used to being alone."

"What kind of work does she do?"

"Before the baby, she had her own catering business. She had a special arrangement with a nearby restaurant, where she cooked when they were closed each night. Meaning, she cooked and baked from like midnight to six in the morning most days. However, with the birth of Little Calum, she's only working from home. No more catering gigs. But she branched out from the one to several related businesses." He gave Damon a proud smile. "She's very entrepreneurial."

CHAPTER 7

M ARIANA WAS IN her room when Little Calum woke up. After a cuddle they played a little card game, and, when he asked for snacks, she made popcorn enough for them all and left the bulk of it in the kitchen, as she and her son returned to their quarters and waited for the guys to return.

She was doing her best to appear as normal as possible for the sake of her son. But even Little Calum knew she was under stress.

"Are you okay, Mommy?"

"I'm fine, sweetheart." He nodded, and they continued to play. Then he asked sheepishly, "Is Daddy coming?"

"Yes, Daddy is coming home soon."

He brightened. "When?"

"I don't know exactly, but he will be here soon," she replied, hoping he wouldn't be too late. Little Calum nodded and didn't say anything more. She didn't know what to say either.

If Little Calum asked, how was she even supposed to explain the situation? But maybe he didn't need any explanation; maybe he was just okay with it all. At least she could hope so anyway. There was just so much going on right now that she didn't know how to do any of this. It's not exactly in a parent's guidebook to deal with stuff fit for the latest fiction stories.

And then why would it be? She'd done everything she could, with the goal of spending more time with Cal, whenever he got out of this scenario, but that didn't mean he would see it the same way. When she heard a commotion outside, she froze in fear.

Little Calum reached over with his chubby little hand, then patted hers. "It's okay, Mommy. It's Daddy."

She stared at him in shock. "What?"

He looked up at her with solemn four-year-old eyes. "It's Daddy," he murmured. "He's back."

She swallowed. "How do you know that? That noise could have been made by anyone," she whispered.

"I just know," he said, with an air of confidence that took her completely off guard. That was the first inkling she had that maybe there was something more to her son than she had realized. But then, of course, it always really was a possibility, since both she and Cal had latent abilities.

Little Calum was most likely as gifted and as brilliant as his father. She had never questioned the validity of Cal's skills or of their value to a team like Terk's—though she knew Cal had gone through a difficult time over making the decision to join them. But, when it came down to it, Cal knew what he needed to do, and he'd gone and done it. The fact that it hadn't included her hadn't changed the fact that she admired him for having the courage and the sense of sacrifice to make that decision for the good of the world.

She wished it had been different, but she wouldn't hold it against him now. Not when they had so much more living to do and owed it to their son to live respectably. Now she had to tell Cal that something more was here than either of them knew—that their son was brilliant beyond belief. As she considered her family's future, as Little Calum crawled up onto her lap, maybe Cal would recognize the value here too of all three of them staying together, using their gifts together.

She shook her head. "Don't be an idiot," she said to herself. *Of course there's value, but safety seems to override all that. I fear he wants to go back to the same situation as before—living separately.*

Her mind was running all likely scenarios, and it was frustrating as hell. She wasn't ready to go back to that prior life, and she wouldn't go for any more half-hearted relationships.

It's all or nothing, Cal.

And it looked very much like the situation they were in. It could very well wind up being nothing. She stared down at her son, feeling tears rising in the back of her eyes.

"It's okay, Mommy," Little Calum said, without looking up. "We'll be fine."

"Yeah?" she replied, with a smile. "I'm glad you think so."

He raised his head and shook it. "I don't think so. I *know* so." And he went back to his cards. When the bedroom door opened, she looked up to see Calum and quickly tried for a smile. But she didn't need to worry because her son was already off the bed and racing for him, crying out, "Daddy!"

Calum immediately swung him up into his arms and held him close. He looked over at her with a questioning eye, and she shook her head. "Welcome back," she murmured.

He nodded slowly. "How's this guy doing?"

"I'm doing good," Little Calum stated proudly. "I just finished playing cards with Mommy, and I won."

"Of course you did. You're a smart man."

"Yep, I'm really smart, aren't I, Mom?"

"Yes, baby," she replied, then looked at Calum. "He's an *exceptionally* smart young man," she stated, with a wry tone. Cal looked at her, and she nodded. *He may well be smarter than everyone here, but I'm not telling him that.*

Cal looked down at his son. But the little guy was far too interested in hearing about Cal's day.

"What did you do?" Little Calum asked. "Are you back now? Can we eat again?"

"Of course you can eat again," he replied, tossing her another look.

"Calum, if you were that hungry, I could have made something other than the popcorn. You barely touched it. Why didn't you say something?"

"I waited because I wanted to eat with Daddy," he said.

And that was another inkling that life would never be the same again. Now that Little Calum had gotten the chance to spend real time interacting with his father, that wasn't something he was prepared to let go of.

She stood, slowly walked over, wrapped her arm around Cal, then whispered, "I guess that means you don't get to go loose," she murmured.

He stiffened ever-so-slightly, but Little Calum chortled and wrapped his arms around his Daddy's neck. "Got you, Daddy!"

"Nope, I got you!" Cal hugged his son close. "Let's go see about that food, *huh*? I'm hungry too."

"Yay!" The little boy squealed with delight, and, with that, they turned and headed to the hallway. At the door, he looked back at her. "Are you coming?"

She nodded slowly. "I'll be out in a minute. I just have to use the washroom."

At that Little Calum piped up. "She needs to cry."

She sucked in her breath. "Calum, why would you say that?"

He shrugged. "Because you do. You get that funny tight look on your face, when something isn't right, when the tears have to come out."

"I see," she said. "I didn't realize you'd noticed." Her son gave her a bland stare that was so much like his father's that she didn't even know what to say. She just waved them off. "Go spend some time together. I'm coming." And, with that, they left.

She slowly walked into the bathroom and sat down, wondering just what had happened. How would she deal with the bond rapidly developing between father and son if Cal decided he didn't want her as part of the package deal?

She couldn't think of anything that would break her heart more, but nothing was guaranteed here. Not for her and not for her son.

"JUST BECAUSE YOU think something like that, and you *know*," Cal cautioned his son, "sometimes you have to watch what you say because it can be embarrassing for your mom."

"But it's true," Calum argued, looking at him funny. "When we saw you again, you had the same look on your face."

"I did," Cal admitted. "I was worried about you, and I was so happy to see you."

"See? So what difference does it make if Mommy goes and cries?"

"It makes a difference to Mommy." Cal bopped his son's

nose. "You're a handful sometimes, aren't you?"

He shrugged. "Nope, I'm fine." And, with that, he scrambled down from his father's hold and raced over to the kitchen table. He wandered around it. "Is this all there is?"

"What would you like?" he asked his son, while looking around and asking the others, "Where's Terk?"

"He went out to help you guys."

He froze at that. "Why?"

The three women looked at each other and back at him. "Because things sounded a little dicey there," Tasha explained. "And we didn't want anything to happen to you."

"Somebody has to stay here and hold down the fort," he stated in a stern manner. "Tasha, you know that."

"I do know that," she replied in defiance, flipping her hair back. "But I also know that we hadn't heard from either Wade or Gage, and that was a concern as well."

Cal frowned. "Do I need to go out and help them?"

"We don't know yet," she replied. "Assuming you told Terk that you were on your way back, I presume he's out trying to help Wade and Gage now."

"Good God," Cal said. "That's why we have a command post—somebody who keeps track of everything." His glare wasn't directed just at Tasha but at all three of them. "If we are to function as a unit, it has to be a functioning unit. It can't just be people going off and doing their own thing, or Terk being afraid of facing you guys if something happened to us."

At that, the women had the grace to look ever-so-sheepish.

"Seriously? Terk is an integral part of this team. Without him, we are all lost." Cal nodded his head for emphasis.

At that, Tasha nodded slowly. "And I do know that, Cal.

But, at the time, we were all really worried about you. It was something Mariana said, about the sister being involved."

"I do know about the sister being involved, but, by then, by the time we went back to her house, she wasn't there," he told them. "We found no sign of her."

"That doesn't mean much," Tasha noted. "Also you need to know that, before you guys woke up, each of us also came under attack, and Terk was even more shorthanded than he is now. We've had to step up and do more than ever before. Things are just different now, in many ways."

"Wow, I knew some of that, but not all," Cal admitted, but just then his phone rang. He checked the screen ID. "Terk, ... where are you?"

"It doesn't matter. I heard from Wade, and they're on their way back."

"So, it was basically a trip for nothing." Cal grunted, raising his eyebrows at the women.

"Right." Terk went on, "I did just hear from Merk."

"And? What did he have to say?"

"Did you check out the shrubbery on the back side of the house?"

"Yeah, that's where I was hiding," Calum replied.

"Well, another body was found."

"*Uh-oh*," Cal said.

"Yeah, this one is still alive, but she's in bad shape."

"Oh, crap." Cal rubbed his head. "I didn't even think to go back there."

"Why would you, if that's where you came from?"

"But we did search the house for her and finally assumed she took off. Her car was gone, or at least I assumed it was her car. Shit." He paused. "Okay, fine. I'm on my way back out there."

"Don't bother," Terk noted. "Merk is sending as much information as he can over to Tasha for analysis."

"Okay, we'll need to tear it apart." He looked over at Tasha and asked, "Did you get any new intel from Merk?"

"It's just coming up now," she replied quietly, pointing to her computer station, as the documents were beginning to open on the screen, and the printer started to run.

"We need to find a connection between Sean, David— Sean's brother who was killed earlier—and their sister, Tay," he shared, with a hard glare at the others, "and the other cases."

"We're already on it," Tasha replied. "We're doing our jobs, Cal."

And, at that, Sophia sat down beside her. "I get that you're angry, Calum," Sophia added. "But honestly, we'd do it again if we had to. There is more at stake now than ever."

He stared at her in shock. Something else was going on here that he didn't quite understand, but, whatever it was, the whole game was changing. They weren't just employees anymore; they were teammates, carrying the safety of their loved ones on their shoulders. They were doing this to protect them all. He also noticed they were armed. He could hardly yell and scream at them for breaking ranks.

"I see," he said, when he got his temper back under control. "But we'll all end up dead if we don't establish some semblance of order and control in this. No more sending people off half-cocked to the field, especially the someone who holds this team together."

"Is he on his way back now? The half-cocked one?" Tasha asked, with a smirk, while she kept an eye on two big screens, one searching for data, another searching the outer perimeter of the warehouse they were in.

"Yeah." Cal sighed. "Jesus, whatever you do, don't tell him I said that, ... please. I'm obviously not up to speed on all the changes since I was in that coma. So ... anything jump out in the data?"

"I'm on that right now," Tasha replied. "I've been trying to figure out what was going on, but this Sean guy seems like he was almost broke."

"He was broke. That's why he was living with his sister."

She looked at him in shock. "All the more reason we should see a large deposit recently."

"What are you suggesting? That he did this for free?" Cal frowned.

"Now that is something I don't know yet," Tasha replied.

"I sure don't want to think that he had so much hate inside him that he was prepared to ... do *that*"—Cal glanced at his son to see if he was listening—"but, if they gave him that opening, I suppose they could have tormented him with it," he guessed. "Or, who knows, maybe his payout would come afterward."

"I think that's probably more likely," Tasha stated, "but I can tell you that he definitely had no money in the bank. All his accounts were empty. I think there's like seven dollars and forty-two cents in his main one."

"Okay, that's beyond broke," he noted. She nodded. "How did he even put gas in the vehicle?"

"Unless the sister hooked him up with cash," Tasha suggested.

Cal cocked his head. "She might have." He was feeling sorry for Sean at that point. "What about the other brother?"

"His finances looked more normal. Like a guy who gets a regular paycheck and takes care of business."

"So, if both brothers are gone, who else gets any estate money? If she's not in their wills, which she may or may not be, maybe she thought to preempt it and get something for herself first?" he asked.

"What are the chances that she was doing all of this to specifically get something for herself?" Tasha asked, looking over at him.

"I don't know the answer to that. I do know they aren't a warm and cozy family. Yet, if she thought Sean was going down or needed to go down, then she might very well have set him up." Cal nodded. "I really hate to think that way, but I saw a side of her today that I would never have expected."

"Yeah, it kind of goes along with the business though, doesn't it?" she asked.

Just then Sophia yelled, "Got it! I found another bank account, and funds are pending but not fully transferred."

"Probably one of those *hold until completion of the job* deals," he noted. "And, in this case, the funds will never fully transfer because the job didn't get completed. Are there any other transfers, or can you track that one?" He stopped, then looking over at Sophia, he asked, "Since it's pending, can you see where it'll reverse to?"

"Well, not legally, … but let me just pop on my hacking hat and see what I can come up with." She grinned at the thought. "I guess that would be the biggest help at this point, wouldn't it?"

"Well, if we could figure out where the money is coming from, we've got a shot at finding out who is paying for it," he said excitedly, walking up behind her. As she went through the databases, he shook his head. "Somebody has to be paying for this. Even if Tay was expecting to take the money and run, somebody shot her and put her down."

"But if they didn't finish the job—"

"Right, and I don't know how bad it is, but that's where Merk is right now." Cal sent Merk a text. **How bad is Tay hurt?**

The response came back immediately. **Fatal.**

"Shit." He looked at the two women. "She's dead.'

"Well, that's an entire family wiped out."

"I know, and a part of me feels responsible." Just then Mariana's voice caught him from the doorway.

"You'd be completely wrong about that, Calum," she said. "That woman was not innocent."

He looked up at her, then frowned. "You didn't know her."

"That is true. I may not know her," she confirmed, "but a woman's instincts are not always some frivolous knowledge," she argued pointedly.

He winced because he had made that comment about Mariana's instincts years before, and she clearly hadn't forgotten. Calum looked over at her, then smiled. "You know that I've always respected your instincts."

"Yet you seem to be incredibly insecure about them."

He winced, rubbing at his face. "I was afraid that you had figured out what I was doing," he admitted, "like somehow you seem to know. I was still pretty new to this stuff, but I was fascinated and desperately wanted more training in it."

"Oh, I remember, but I never doubted that you believed in them."

He nodded slowly. "So, what are you talking about right now?"

CHAPTER 8

"**M**Y INSTINCTS SAY that, if Tay wasn't involved, she sure as hell wasn't helping your side either." Mariana stared at Cal, studying him.

"Well, whatever her faults, it doesn't matter at this point."

"For that, I am very sorry," she replied quietly. "None of us need to come to that kind of end. But, at the same time, if she had anything to do with this, and with the kidnapping of me and endangering our son," she stated a little loudly, "I would just as soon she was gone. I know that's a hard way to look at it, but I don't want to be looking over my shoulder and wondering about every woman who's out there."

"You know that Tay and I hadn't had a relationship in a very long time, right?"

"I know she was before me," Mariana stated flatly, "but that doesn't change much."

"It changes a lot—in many ways," he replied firmly. "She wasn't you."

"No, but it apparently doesn't matter," she said, then shrugged. "You left her too."

"Yes, I did," he admitted, then looked back at the other women and raised both hands, showing his palms. "This is not exactly a conversation I want to have with an audience."

"We're all in pretty tight confines," Mariana replied

coolly. "So the conversations will come up at that community level whether we like it or not."

"I get it. Honestly, I do, and I'm sorry."

She smiled. "Of course you are, but, at the same time, if she had something to do with this—"

"I hope not," he replied. "I really hope her soul hadn't been corrupted to that degree, but we don't really know what people are like until they hit a hardship, and then you see who shows up for the challenge. That was a kind of convoluted way of saying that a person's true character shows up in times of adversity."

She seemed to get it anyway. "I wouldn't be at all surprised." Then she turned, and her eyes widened in horror. "Little Calum, what are you eating?"

Cal looked over to see his son with his whole fist inside the peanut butter jar. There was no spoon, no bread, just his fist coming out of the jar and into his mouth.

"Son," she said, as she raced over. "Other people might want to eat some of that too, you know?" He looked up at her, then looked at his fist completely smeared in peanut butter and offered it to her.

At that, Cal burst out laughing and joined them. "How about a slice of bread with that, buddy?"

Little Calum grinned at him. "Sure."

And, with that, Cal made his son a sandwich. No one else watched, except for Mariana, who had grabbed a washcloth and had picked up Little Calum and carried him over to the sink, where she was working hard to find the skin underneath all that peanut butter. "Please tell me that it's not in your hair too," she moaned.

He just smiled at her. "I like peanut butter."

"I know you like peanut butter, sweetheart, but other

people here eat it too. So next time, we'll spread it on a slice of bread."

"It takes too long. Besides, it's all going into my tummy."

She sighed. "I know, but you need to use better manners than that," She looked over at Cal. "You do realize you're partially responsible for this."

He stared at her in shock. "Me? Why am I responsible?" he asked, half laughing and half serious.

"You're the peanut butter guy. I can't stand the stuff, but Little Calum eats it all the time."

"It's good for him," Cal stated.

"Sure, but he needs more than just peanut butter. I knew we would have no problems at all feeding him, when I saw you had a big jar of it here."

"Well, it's kind of a staple for some of us," Cal admitted.

She laughed and smiled. "That's what Wade said, and I guess it's true for Little Calum as well. Even though he hasn't seen you eat it, he's just as addicted to the stuff as you are." She added, "I'd prefer a stir-fry myself."

"And, if we had the ability to cook here, we could all pitch in and do that," Cal stated. "But, until we get clearance to access the rest of the building, that's not likely to happen."

She stopped to look at him. "Is that part of the plan? To get the rest of the building?"

"Yes. We need the space."

She nodded. "We sure do." Then she looked down at her son and said, "Now, if you're ready to sit nicely, I'll put you back over at the table, and you can have your sandwich."

He beamed up at her. "Daddy made me a sandwich," he said, as she put him back in the chair.

Calum handed the sandwich over to his son. "Here you

go, buddy."

Little Calum looked at it, took a bite, and then held it up. "Do you want a bite too?"

Cal smiled. "You know something, bud, I can't think of anything I'd like more right now." And he sat down and split the peanut butter sandwich with his son.

If there was ever anything guaranteed to make a woman cry, it was the sight of a man bonding with his son, like Cal was doing right now. Something was just so special about the two of them in this moment that brought tears to her eyes. Mariana barely brushed them away before either of them saw, but she also knew that her son was a little too perceptive and would call her out on it. Thankfully he was distracted by his father.

She cleaned up the rest of the peanut butter mess that he had managed to get on his shirt and, yes, even in his hair. While he ate, she quickly wiped at strands of his hair. She looked at the shirt and groaned, then wiped off what little bit she could. She turned to Cal. "We'll need some more clothes, although I gave Terk a list earlier."

"I'm sure we can do something about that," Cal replied, as he patted his son's cheek. "I'll have a second sandwich."

"Me too," Little Calum said immediately.

Cal made two more sandwiches, and, as they sat here, she looked at the both of them. "You know that I need more than that for a meal, right?"

He pointed at the table. "Well, unless Terk's bringing home some food, this could be dinner tonight."

"Fine." She looked around and made herself a sandwich with deli meat and lots of fresh veggies. When she offered a bite to her son, he just shook his head and held up his sandwich.

"Again, that's not your fault. Shit happens, and it doesn't necessarily mean it's got anything to do with you."

And, while Cal heard the words and agreed with them, they didn't help his mood much. With the officers working outside, he asked, "Are we allowed back in the house?"

"Yes," he replied. "I'm here kind of on loan, if you will. We can't take anything, and we have to share everything we find, but we do have clearance. Ice and Levi have some exceptional connections within MI6."

"I'm sure the locals don't trust us though."

"Would you?" he asked, with a smile.

"No," he replied, "not for a moment."

"So don't be surprised if that is the kind of response we get."

Cal nodded. "Let's go take a look." As they walked back into the house, he told Merk, "Back at headquarters, we're wondering how the communication worked between these guys and Sean. Like how they would have known that this guy hated me, what method they used to contact him, and what inducements they used to get him to do this?"

"Inducements wouldn't have been much, since he was already primed," Merk noted. "So, the next issue is how did they know that Sean was somebody who wanted you dead? Or wanted you guys annihilated one way or another?"

"That would be of interest to me as well," Cal admitted. "Unless they kept the levels compartmentalized, so nobody knew too much."

"Yeah, that is possible too," Merk admitted. "It's just so damn frustrating with all our potential witnesses already dead."

"It is, but, instead of being frustrated, let's get down to work and find something concrete we can do something about." And, with that, they started through the house. "This was her house?" Cal asked Merk.

"Yes. It was once their parents' house," he explained. "And it was left, I assume, to the two of them—or all of the siblings maybe. She had been living here and had just recently let Sean come back to live here."

"Okay, we'll get somebody to confirm the details of ownership—not that it makes much difference right now. Unless of course," he said, looking over at Merk, "unless somebody is after the house."

He stopped, looked at him, and nodded. "That is another angle to consider, but it doesn't sound like that would have anything to do with our case, since it seems like our guys are pretty well-heeled."

"They might be well funded, but that doesn't mean they would be against having yet another base from which to operate."

"That's a possibility too," Merk replied, with a nod.

Something else to consider.

And, with that, they kept walking through the house. At her bedroom, Cal stopped, then winced. "This feels like such an invasion of privacy."

"Were you ever in this house?"

"Up until about a couple of hours ago, when I was searching for her, no," he replied. "Her parents were still alive when I knew her. And they were living here."

"And you never met them?"

Cal shook his head. "No, I never did. So maybe that's a blessing too," he murmured. He shrugged. "I don't know. All of this just seems so strange."

"Yeah, I get that," Merk agreed. "At the same time, until we get down to the bottom of it all, we have to keep an open mind."

An open mind was one thing, but walking through an ex-girlfriend's home, wondering what she had been up to and how involved she had been in the kidnapping of his wife and son was something else. "Another thing I don't understand," Cal shared, "is how they would have even known about Mariana."

"I've been wondering that same thing about all you guys. It would be good to find out how much is in your personnel files. Plus, I'm wondering how much they've tapped into all your phones."

"It shouldn't have been possible," Cal replied.

At that, Merk took a slow deep breath. "Unless ... somebody on the inside was helping them."

Calum stopped and stared. "I really don't like the sound of that."

"No, I'm sure you don't, and we've already lost the one defense department operative," he noted. "But these guys may not have had access to the innermost details of the way you guys work."

"Nobody does, and really the only person who knows everything is Terk," he pointed out.

"I get that," he confirmed, "and we all know that Terk wouldn't have had anything to do with this."

"No, he wouldn't have, but it doesn't change the fact that some scenarios here look a little on the murky side."

"Do you trust Lorelei?" Merk asked.

Calum thought about it and nodded, first a bit unsurely, and then more forcefully. "Yes, I do."

"Okay, that's worth a lot too." Merk nodded. "What about anybody else?"

"Sophia, absolutely," Cal added. "She is a little more of a

wild card for us than the others, but she also comes from your company."

"And we've taken a pretty hard look at her many times over, just to be sure," he shared, "and she keeps coming up clean. And her association within your group, of course, is Wade."

Cal nodded at that. "I don't think she would do anything to put his life in danger. Which, as you know, there's a lot to be said for that type of relationship that can keep you safe," he murmured.

"Unless it's leading you into believing something that doesn't exist," he pointed out. He walked over to Tay's night table.

"I still can't believe she's in the middle of this mess." Cal shook his head, contemplating something else entirely. "There have been so many deaths and crazy twists and turns that I need to make sure these people are actually dead. Especially Sean, David, Tay. Even Wilson and Mera."

"Well, I think the coroner is still out there, so, maybe before they take off, you can take a quick look at photos of who they've got and how they were identified."

"You mean, a positive ID and all that?" he asked. "Sean's been threatening me for so long, it's hard to imagine he's gone. We were friends at one time."

"Yeah, and what about the girl?"

Cal shrugged. "We broke up years ago."

"Any regrets?"

"No." The answer was instinctive, fast. Calum was relieved at some level here. "She started to get too possessive. A bit crazy, considering how my life works, and we did part on amicable terms. Hell, I even thought it was mutual, until today."

Merk immediately shook his head. "You know what? I hear people say that all the time, but I always wonder if people really understand what it means."

"Well, let me say that I got no arguments out of her when I told her that I wanted to break up, and the first words out of her mouth were, 'Good, I was trying to figure out how to say the same thing to you.'"

Merk looked at him in surprise, then shrugged.

"So, maybe it was what I thought, or"—Cal paused— "she was really just saving her ego in the moment. I think, if she had gotten into another decent relationship not long afterward, our breakup may not have been an issue at all. But apparently she couldn't find anybody else who appealed in all this time, which seems unlikely."

Merk nodded. "There's always that possibility of the *think about the one who got away* issue."

"Maybe, but I'm not sure if it's a case of the one who got away as much as wondering what it was about her that wasn't enough or something."

"Did she have insecurities along that line?"

"Does anybody ever really know?" Cal murmured right back at him. "I wouldn't have thought so, but who the hell knows."

"Good enough," Merk replied. "Now let's get this place searched quickly, before we lose our opportunity to be in here."

And, with that, they checked the house thoroughly, room by room.

"We need to grab phones, laptops, and any smart device capable of storing information," Cal noted.

"You won't see any of that, and I am almost certain we won't likely see a laptop." They kept searching, and finally they did find something at the bottom of the closet.

Merk pulled out a box, which contained an old briefcase. As soon as he opened it, he said, "Voilà, how about an old laptop?"

"And why would you keep an old one?" Calum murmured.

"Lots of people do. Just kind of a spare, in case something happens until they can get a new one or something. Maybe she wanted to wipe it first. I don't know," Merk said. "I guess it's a long shot." He booted it up, and it turned on okay, which was a blessing, considering it was definitely an older model. As he brought up the internet, he opened up the emails tab and muttered, "She doesn't even have security on it."

"Which means she didn't use it for anything important." Cal shrugged. "But remember. She wasn't exactly the kind of person who I would have said was into, you know, stealthy secretive stuff."

"I get it," Merk replied.

"So is anything there or not?" Calum asked.

Merk checked through and shook his head. "A lot of it's just been deleted." Then he checked the Trash folder because not everybody empties that before they store away a laptop. He went through it and nodded. "Definitely a few things of interest in here. Can we send this to Ice or to one of your team?"

Cal said, "Let's send it to both, just in case."

Merk zipped the contents of the Trash and sent it off for an extensive forensics search by Ice and Stone, plus Sophia. Merk looked through the rest of the laptop meanwhile.

So Cal checked Tay's email screen and noted, "It's her same email account."

"Which means any new emails will be there too, and as it's"—Merk checked the notification screen—"it's updating them, and it'll probably take a bit. I wonder if we can take this away with us."

"I doubt it," Cal replied.

"No, of course not. More so, they'll want this too."

"We do need to have whatever information is available copied to us first," Cal noted. "MI6 is trying to solve a murder, but we're trying to stop more murders," he murmured.

While that updated, Merk hunted through the house, looking for anything of value. When he came back into the room a little bit later, he was frustrated as hell. "Is it updated now?" he asked Cal.

"Yes, it just did, and I found lots of very interesting emails. I've changed the password, and I've written down how to get into it for later."

"Okay, that's the best way to do it," he stated. "As long as there is stuff of interest, it will give us time to look."

"I also installed an app that will let me multiforward," Cal shared, "so I'm sending out quite a bit of stuff right now."

"You need to do it in such a way that nobody knows we've taken the stuff," he reminded him.

"Yeah, I got it. I wasn't born yesterday. I'm downloading all of these emails as PDFs." With that done, he cleared both the Trash and the emails in the Inbox. With the new log-in information secure, he put the laptop back into the same place it had been. "I don't know if they'll find it or not."

"I'll tell them it's there. We may get something from them later by cooperating," he added.

"Good enough." And, with that, Cal stood and asked,

"Did you find anything else?"

Merk shrugged. "A few things, yeah. I wanted you to come take a look." With that, he motioned them into the spare bedroom, and Cal stopped, noting it was just like he had seen not too long ago, when he was searching for Tay. But now? Now he looked at it differently, as clues. The mess still was everywhere. Dirty clothes were on the floor, mixed in with clean ones, and some still were on hangers. The floor on the right-hand wall was littered with shoes, and everywhere papers were crumpled up and cast about. Piles of tissues were discarded on the left side of the bed.

"This is Sean's room," Cal said instantly.

"I was thinking that and wondered if you had the same thought."

"Tay, when I knew her, was very neat and tidy," Cal noted quietly. "This isn't her style at all."

"Might not be her style, but we also don't know what her mental state was like these days. Like what's with all the tissues?"

"No, that's true," he murmured, as he looked around. "Yet this is all men's clothing, and it definitely doesn't look like her."

"Okay, good enough," Merk said. "And, if that's the case, we really need to sort through anything of value here." But, even as they looked, it was hard to see anything useful.

"Where's his phone?" Cal asked. "And more than his phone, where's his laptop? I don't see any communication devices of any kind."

"I don't know," Merk murmured. "The phone wasn't on the body. I didn't see anything over at the neighbor's house either, where he used their balcony for his sniper location."

"You've already been there?"

Merk nodded. "I went in there first," he said, and then he hesitated but thought better than to withhold information. "I don't know if you know this, but he killed the neighbors too. A husband and wife, ... both in their seventies."

Cal stared back, feeling more sorry than shocked. "No, I didn't know that for certain, though he made some reference about the neighbor not minding the noise. Do you think Sean killed them or was it the person who killed Sean?"

"We won't know any of that just yet," he murmured. "I just thought you should know."

"Yeah, thanks," he said in a distant tone. He shook his head. "It could just as easily have been Sean. He was quite cocky in our conversation."

"As if he was *the man* and had finally found his true self?" Merk asked in a hard voice.

Calum thought about it, then nodded. "Something like that, yeah. I know it doesn't sound normal but—"

"Nothing is normal about these guys," he murmured. "That's one of those lessons we have to remember. They're picking people who know you, Cal. They are picking people who are obviously disturbed in some way and egging them on to help them put you down."

"But I still don't understand how they had access to my information."

"Did you ever mention Mariana to anybody?"

He shook his head. "A few years ago, I might have said something, but I wouldn't have expected anybody to have remembered that." He frowned. "I've barely had any contact with her—other than sending money." Then he stopped and shook his head. "No, that's not completely true. I've tried to visit a couple times a year to see my son."

"So what are the chances you were tracked? Followed? Phone numbers or the money traced—or all of the above?"

He nodded slowly. "I guess that's possible. I did take precautions, but I never even told the guys. Terk knew a little, but that's all. We were ... I was just taking a few days to go visit."

"Of course," he said in understanding. "And were they just visits to see the boy or maybe something more?"

"Meaning?"

"Were you also trying to keep the relationship alive for another day?"

He shrugged. "Let me just say that, every time I saw her and realized that she still hadn't moved on, I felt more encouraged that I would get a second chance."

"And don't you think she knew that? Don't you think that she was holding on and hoping for that as well?"

"Yes, I do," he admitted quietly. "But I also knew it wasn't fair to her. This was just all so crazy. We lived in the present, in a lifestyle that I couldn't see how it would ever end, but then I knew it would, when suddenly we were shut down. And that was it. I was looking forward to sweeping her off her feet, but then we were attacked and ..." Calum trailed off a bit.

At that, Merk nodded. "And that makes total sense. If you think about it, there is only so much time and effort any asshole is willing to put into killing you guys. If they had a perfect opportunity, they might have moved the time line up."

"Honestly, we were thinking that they may have had a part in the timeline. And we're really not out of the woods yet," he noted.

"I know you're all thinking that it was the government

that did this," Merk stated. "And believe me. We're not discounting that because we've seen way too many things like that happen. But Terk's team is something that nobody even knows about. Nobody, not even the defense department, knows that you're functioning on these other levels."

"Except for Bob, our handler. Not that he knew everything, ... but he knew enough that he was the first one executed."

Merk nodded, while frowning. "Okay then. That raises a red flag, yet still Bob didn't know what Terk knows."

"No, and I get that, but these guys after us, if they got to Bob and had a partial look at us, then they also should have been a little better prepared to take us out, if that were the plan. And these guys do seem to know us better than that."

"Did you ever consider that maybe they hired somebody?"

He looked at him in surprise. "Some other DOD operative or special ops team?"

"Maybe a contract killing through somebody else. And maybe that somebody else had a better idea as to what kind of death it should be."

Calum went silent, thinking about that for a moment. Something occurred to him, and he stopped to turn around and look at Merk. "You know something? If we all had stayed in a coma, it would have been like a living death."

"And, therefore," Merk said, following Cal's train of thought, "somebody might think it was a fate worse than death for you."

He slowly nodded. "And it would be, if we weren't healing from that mess," he noted. "If the other guys experienced the coma like me, where I was cognizant mentally, if from afar, then too much more of that and I'd have broken down."

Merk hesitated, then asked, "Like *floating above your body* things?"

Cal shook his head. "That would have been too detached, too separated from the problem—which might have been easier to cope with. No. It was more ... *immersive*, like what I suppose the opposite of Alzheimer's is. With senility, it seems your body is present, but your mind isn't always. And you're not aware that you've forgotten when in that state. Yet I was fully aware that my body had been taken from me—if that makes sense." He shrugged. "If we weren't slowly getting our minds back properly, it would be worse than death."

Merk shook his head. "In which case, ... somebody who put out the contract would have assumed the job was done, but, as you guys began to resurface, they realized that the job wasn't done well enough after all and that you could potentially be cracking down on whoever had the original contract, ultimately getting to whoever was behind it."

"And again all that is plausible. It's just that we have no proof. And every time we turn around, it seems like we're out in the weeds and getting farther and farther away from that."

"Well, whoever is trying to finish the job now may be looking for a more creative way to do it, maybe?" Merk suggested.

"Define *creative?*"

"Something that keeps them a little farther at a distance. Or maybe they did what they wanted to do initially, in that first attack, and now someone doesn't give a shit anymore about you guys in comas but wants dead bodies," he suggested, throwing up his hands. "I mean, with people like this, there's just no way to know."

"I know. I get it." Cal straightened his shoulders and rotated his neck. "I just want to make sure this is over and then head back."

"Will you try to take your son out to the park?"

"I can't believe they took him out in the first place," Cal noted. "I mean, if somebody is tracking us, what the hell?"

"And yet, according to Terk, you guys have ways and means of keeping everybody safe."

"If we had that same means of keeping everyone safe, then why the hell did we all go down in the first place?" Immediately Cal held up his hand. "I know. ... Don't answer that. It's just my frustration talking. None of us would even be alive right now without Terk, and we know it."

Merk laughed. "Hey, believe me. We're all in a similar boat. Terk is very important to us all."

"Ditto. I wouldn't be where I am without him," Cal murmured. "I was an operative, slowly going crazy. And Terk straightened me up, cleaned me up, fixed me up, and showed me that I wasn't going crazy, but that I did have abilities that I had been ignoring."

"Yeah, my brother is good at that," Merk confirmed, with a smile. "The fact that he even found you guys is what blows me away. I sometimes wondered if you didn't put out a call or something. You know, like psychics anonymous or something."

"Hey, that's not bad," Cal noted on a chuckle, "but I don't know. Like, how did we all just fall into Terk's world?"

"I don't think it was a case of falling into his world as much as he was on the hunt for you."

"Exactly, but how do you hunt for somebody like us?"

"The personnel files, maybe? If someone hacked in, they'd find all kinds of information. Most of it's shit I wouldn't want anyone to know about. How about you?" Merk looked at him. "How much trouble were you in?"

"I was constantly in trouble," he admitted, "but I didn't think it was that bad."

"I wonder if you might want to have somebody double-check what 'that bad' actually means."

"*Great.* Maybe we should. Maybe that's the only information source that these guys have. Do you think?"

"No, let me stop you right there," Merk said. "Forget all that. … Just ask Terk outright. He'll tell you."

Calum kept that thought in mind, as he headed back to headquarters. Anything was better than remembering the body. It had definitely been Tay.

One bullet hole in the back of her head, with the front of the face partially exploded, but there was no mistaking the rest of her. And now here he was, heading home. Funny how a warehouse of all places could so quickly become home.

Knowing that he still had an awful lot to make up for, he had some hard questions for Terk. And Cal also knew that Mariana would have some hard questions for him. And was he prepared to answer them? Because, if he wasn't, this would be a done deal very quickly. And he would do anything to not lose them.

Both of them.

CHAPTER 9

MARIANA STARED AT the screen in front of her. "Jesus Christ," she whispered in a low voice.

"I told you," Tasha said, "and I'm sorry." She looked over at Lorelei. "That's really good work."

Lorelei, still shaking from what she'd found, lifted her cup of coffee and nodded. "Thanks. Too bad I didn't find it earlier."

Tasha shrugged. "We've got it now. As soon as the men are back, we'll have a powwow about this."

"Well, some of us are back," Terk replied, "particularly whenever we hear something like this in your voices. What's going on?"

"Lorelei went and found us a big fish." Tasha then stopped, looked over at Lorelei. "You better explain it yourself."

"Okay, sure. I've been hunting steadily for any information that Bob in DOD, your agency handler, may have had that could have been exposed. It bothered me to think that anybody could know about Mariana. It was the private parts of our lives that concerned me, and that's just too much varied private stuff for anybody to have labeled as casual information," she noted, "and it's obviously not in any of your personnel files." She took a deep breath.

"Somehow they still got to Mariana, so I was looking for

a clue as to how that could have happened. I worked using the assumption that the team and Calum were doing everything possible to protect them."

At that, Mariana nodded. "I know he did," she replied, "very little contact, and the visits were not very often or consistent at all. I wanted and needed for his son to see Cal more, but he was adamant, and obviously I didn't have a clue how crazy this could all get."

"Nobody could, Mariana," Lorelei confirmed.

"If you weren't part of the inner workings of this team, how could you possibly know?" Tasha asked.

With a grateful smile at the reassurance from these women, who were quickly becoming her friends, Mariana shrugged.

Lorelei continued. "It just felt wrong, so I went back into the DOD ops files and eventually found something buried under encryption that you really need to see."

"So, you're saying that Bob was keeping a much more in-depth personnel file on everyone?" Terk asked.

She nodded. "Yes, on everyone, and stuff in here is quite concerning about all of us. Not me, per se, although I'm not sure when this was created."

"So, nobody knew about you then?"

"Maybe. I'm hoping not," she said, with a wince. "This stuff is kind of hard to see. This isn't exactly a black-and-white situation here, and it's pretty clear that somebody has been dissecting your lives."

"How would Bob have gotten this information?" Terk asked, needing to understand it better.

She shrugged. "It could have been anything, but it would have been something that he probably kept on the down-low. So, maybe he hired an investigator, and perhaps some sort of file was opened on everybody. That way, anytime anybody took a flight, it was recorded here"—she pointed—"and flights from Paris to London have been noted in Cal's record." She looked over at Mariana. "Were you ever there with Cal?"

Mariana nodded. "Yes. I went to visit my family in London," she stated. "And one of the times when he came to see me was there. You guys were in Paris at the time."

Lorelei nodded. "And Bob has a record of that."

Terk came up behind Lorelei. "We'll need copies of everything in those files. And we need to make sure this can't be forwarded to anybody else."

"I'm working on downloading everything there. These were secret files," she repeated. "They weren't open to anybody, and it has taken me this long to crack it. I'm sorry about that," she said, looking up at Terk. "We really could have used this information a lot earlier."

He shook his head. "Don't even go there right now. It's great that you've found it. We've got it now, and that will give us an awful lot more to work with," he noted forcefully.

She certainly needed no additional motivation.

"Can you retrieve the names of anyone who accessed this information? Is there a way to check the logs, emails, and any accounts that can be linked in any way to the original file?"

"It's just under Bob's name," she replied. "I mean, I can't say for sure that he did anything with this information. All I can tell you is that the file exists."

"And he's a spook—*was* a spook," Tasha noted quietly to Terk. "Remember that. Everybody is suspicious, and everybody is hypervigilant. Everybody keeps track of everything, but that doesn't mean he did anything in particular with this info."

Terk nodded slowly. "But, if anybody even knew this file existed, it might have been a reason to kill him, and he was taken out almost as soon as the accident happened. He was initially considered the primary target in the attack that took the rest of us out."

"I wondered about that." Lorelei seemed exhausted. "I'm still trying, but it doesn't tell me if anybody else logged in." She swiveled around. "Oh, wait. Hang on a second. ... There was a log-in on the day of his death."

"But nothing since?"

She shook her head. "Nothing since, so I would assume that they took all the information they needed and had no intention of trying to access it again. Once in, once out, and hope nobody notices."

"Ah, but you did." Terk smiled. "Thank you for that."

She looked up at him. "I don't feel like you owe me thanks, and honestly, I should have seen this before."

"And how would you have known it was there? It wasn't under the normal channels but in some secret file that only he had access to," Terk said.

"There was an odd note in his file with a log-in," she explained, "so I went through his history, and that's when I found the last person who was there."

"And can you tell if it was morning or afternoon?"

"It was at two in the afternoon roughly," she replied.

"So, after Bob's already dead."

She nodded. "Yes." Then she grimaced.

Mariana hated the thoroughness of both the government and her kidnappers, but it gave her a sense of relief to know how she'd been found. "What are the chances that Bob was tortured to give up that file by someone who knew about it and who couldn't take the chance of something like that existing?"

"Or couldn't take the chance of something like that which would incriminate him," Tasha suggested, from the other side of the room.

At that, Terk looked at her. "Are you talking about betrayal?"

Tasha frowned, possibly confused, when she added, "It could be that Bob was considered as part of our team and taken out like the rest of us. However, maybe he was part of the bad guys' team in this whole scenario and has been taken out, just like Sean and the other hires were killed."

"All possible," Terk admitted, as he looked over at Lorelei. "Have you been able to do a run on Bob?"

"Most of his files are blank, which is pretty well standard for the DOD and other security departments. Everything gets locked up behind forty-seven million shields, and, if you really want to find it, then good luck with that."

Terk looked over at Tasha.

She nodded. "I looked too, and nothing's there."

He nodded. "How about financial records? Has anybody looked into that or into life insurance?"

"I've been working on that," Sophia said. "So far we're not finding anything that's really making us sit up and pay attention."

"If it was something like that," Terk noted, "we'd be looking in the wrong place. It'll be something very subtle and very minor. But, like this file of his, it'll have a huge impact. Bob was very paranoid, and we had plenty of arguments about it."

"Did you talk with him much?" Mariana asked curiously. "I wish I knew more about your lives before this attack."

He shook his head. "As to your question, no, I didn't

speak to Bob much and not recently at all. We didn't hit it off very well, though maybe that's another reason why this file exists."

Mariana nodded. "So you didn't like him, and he didn't trust you, which made him start keeping all kinds of bits and pieces on us."

"That's right, and it was one of our arguments," Terk noted. "I just never thought there would be something like this hidden away. I would have thought it would have been in the standard personnel files. The fact that it was collected privately could mean almost anything. But likely nothing."

"It could mean that he was looking to sell the information or maybe it was for his own purpose for getting rid of us down the road. For all you know, it was part of the ammo used to disband the team," Mariana suggested quietly. "I imagine plenty of people who didn't understand all this energy work were in favor of that happening."

"Jesus, are we that unstable that they had to do something like that?" Tasha asked in a half-joking manner.

"I don't know what to think," Terk admitted. "You would hope that anything Bob had that he thought was a viable gripe would have been something that he shared with us, so we could address it."

"Well, maybe he did," Mariana suggested. "And maybe he shared it with the wrong person."

At that, Sophia turned around and frowned. "In that case, … how about we start cross-referencing everybody he worked with, everybody he socialized with, and his phone records, both at work and at home."

Terk nodded. "Good thought. You do that. We never really looked into his connection to this, did we?"

"We've been a little busy avoiding subsequent attacks,"

Tasha noted, "but you're right. We could have gone deeper. We will now." And she turned and headed back to the computers too.

Lorelei looked over at him. "What do you want me to do?"

"Have you downloaded all that information?"

She nodded.

"Delete it," Terk said. "Make sure it's 100 percent gone and scrub it or do whatever you need to do. Just make sure nobody else can get that information. We're already in all the trouble we can handle, so let's not have yet something else out there that can impact our friends and family more than these people have already been."

She asked, "Do you think other people can still use this?"

"I don't know," Terk said honestly, "because I don't know all of what's in there, and I need to. The bottom line is, we have to make sure that whatever we come up against is for our use only."

She nodded, as she got to work.

In a while, she stopped and looked up at him. "Will we do something where this will be needed?"

"I don't know," he replied. "Information is always valuable, which is why everybody collects it. We won't be any different in that sense, but we need to know what the enemy knows about us before we can be sure that we're safe."

"Got it," she stated.

"Will you have trouble doing that?" he asked.

She looked up at him and shook her head. "No, getting rid of the information is a good idea. My question more or less"—she was unsure whether to say it or not—"relates to whether we'll be collecting information on others."

"Maybe," Terk noted. "And I'll ask you again. ... Will that be a problem?"

She frowned. "I don't think so because it's definitely something that we'll potentially need, depending on what we do going forward. All information is valuable, like you said."

He nodded. "So, for the moment, just do what you need to do to make sure nobody else gets it. This is information on us," he noted. "It's likely information on you as well."

She nodded and winced. "Yeah, it sure is. Not as much and not as in-depth, but a lot of other people work for the department as well."

"I'll take a look at it to see if it's relevant. Other than that, we don't want anybody else to have this kind of access."

"I'm still quite stunned that Bob even gathered this," she admitted.

"I'm not. He was very"—he stopped, searching for a proper word for it, then shrugged—"I don't know how to say it nicely, but he was a paranoid asshole."

She laughed. "You do know that many people would say that about you, don't you?"

He grinned. "And you know something? They'd be right. And with good reason."

She nodded.

Mariana had watched the exchange. What it highlighted for her was the sense of being left out, of not being able to contribute. Of having nothing to offer. "So, they have everything on my relationship with Calum?"

Lorelei winced. "They have everything on you, your family, and your son—including his birth date, where he was born, everything," she replied in a very quiet tone.

"So, all that time Calum thought, by staying away, that we would be safe, we were never really safe at all."

"Exactly," Lorelei replied. "Sorry, I know it's upsetting."

"Yeah, well, in this case, it's more ammo."

"More ammo? What does that mean?" Terk asked, as he walked toward her.

She smiled. "More ammo to use as an argument so Calum keeps us around."

"I don't think keeping you around will be the problem," Terk replied.

She shrugged. "I'm not so sure about that. I think he really believes that we would be safer somewhere else."

He nodded. "We always want to pick up and put people where we want them to stay, so that we know that they're protected and secure, but we don't always know that our choices are correct."

"Well, in this case, they weren't." Just then the rear door opened, and Cal walked in. She got up, then walked over and gave him a quick hug. "You look like hell."

"Yeah, I feel like it too," he said, hugging her back. "How's the little guy?"

"He's fine. He's in the other room, with some kind of math game."

"Great." Cal laughed. "He'll be beating me in math pretty damn fast."

"You know what? I don't think you're wrong about that," she replied. "I think he's ... maybe I'm just being a proud mom, but I think he's seriously special."

Cal smiled. "Of course you do."

She laughed. "I know, and I get it. I really do, but I'm also not so sure that I'm wrong."

"As long as you're not projecting it on him, it's all good."

She nodded. "I don't think I am, but I also haven't had

him tested because I want him to have as normal a life as possible."

"Normal would be good," Cal said. "As normal a life as possible, and that includes having a father." He just stared at her. "We can discuss that later."

And, with that, she had to be satisfied. As he went to walk away, she called out, "Just not too much later."

"*Huh?*" He stopped, then frowned and turned back to face her.

"You need to hear about some of the stuff that they've found since you've been away all day," she said.

At that, he faced the others. "Bring me up to speed, please."

Terk stepped up and explained about the secret file. And Mariana watched Cal's expression change from shock to horror, until he slowly turned toward her.

She nodded. "So, all that time you stayed away, thinking you were doing the right thing, … they already knew," she stated.

He just shook his head, speechless.

She got up to walk over to him, reaching out to touch his arm. "Hey, this isn't your fault."

"Who the hell's fault was it then?" He stared at her, his tone harsh.

She winced. "Okay, so if you want to take that on your shoulders, I can't really do anything about it, but all I can tell you is that we're here now. We're safe, and we will get through this."

"We're safe," he said foggily, and suddenly it all came crashing down on him. "Jesus. It came so close to … you not being safe. I'm sorry. I thought—"

"There's got to be a reason why that came to pass," Terk

stated. "Did you ever think about that?"

Calum looked at him and frowned. "So that you guys would rescue her."

"Nobody else was rescued," Terk noted bluntly, "because they didn't want anybody else rescued. So, either she still has a use for them or she's of no value."

"But, of no value is still of value," Calum replied. "They've taken out everybody else, and, for all they know, she has been taken out too."

"Possibly," Terk said, with a nod, "and possibly? ... Possibly she's still of value."

"What?" she asked, shivering at the thought. "What could I possibly offer them?"

"The same thing you always have," Terk noted. "Access to Cal."

She stared at him in shock. "Oh, wow." She looked around, feeling a bit vulnerable.

"Here I was thinking that maybe we needed to find us another place to stay safe because you're getting crowded here," Cal said, "but now I'm thinking I don't want to go too far."

"You're not going very far at all," Terk replied, smiling. "We've been able to rent the rest of this building, so we don't have to worry about relocating for the time being. It's under three different corporations, rented at different times, and paid by different methods, so hopefully we'll fly under the radar for as long as we stay here. So that's not an issue." He smiled at everyone. "Meaning that we now have access to a full commercial kitchen, and there are other bedrooms with bathrooms that we can set up into a suite of rooms for each of you right now."

Mariana looked at Cal and said, "I still need to get some

clothes and other personal items for Little Calum and myself. Thanks to our kidnappers, we arrived with nothing."

"I know. Sorry. We haven't had a spare moment to get that done."

"I've been hoping there would be a window so we could get out and get some air and maybe do some shopping sometime."

"There is." Calum nodded. "We can go right now," he said, as he looked over at Terk.

"And do you think that's a good idea right now?" she asked Terk, realizing that, despite the fact they were all strong and capable men, Terk seemed to have the final answer on everything.

Terk nodded. "Just be alert for trouble," he said to Calum. Then looking over at her, he added, "Be careful."

As Cal hesitated, clearly torn, Wade hopped up and said, "I'm coming along too. Do you mind?"

He looked at his friend with relief and nodded. "That would be good."

"It'll be hard to keep an eye on everybody," Wade stated, looking at her. "Any chance of leaving the little guy at home?"

She hesitated and then nodded. "Only if someone is okay to babysit," she said, looking at the women expectantly.

Immediately Tasha nodded. "Not a problem," she said. "I've got several younger brothers. I've done more than my fair share of babysitting in my time."

"We won't be long," Mariana added hesitantly, "and don't mind the tantrums. Little Calum hasn't had much in the way of babysitters, so I don't know how he'll do."

"Well, let's find out," she suggested.

At that, Little Calum took one look at everyone, and his

face bunched up. Mariana turned to Cal and, in a soft voice, added, "He's still not fully recovered from the kidnapping."

"Hey, buddy, it's fine. We will be back real soon."

"You need to stay with Tasha," Mariana added. "Won't that be great?"

"It's best, buddy, if you stay here," Cal told his son. "I promise we'll both be back soon."

But Little Calum wasn't too interested in hearing it.

Cal looked at the boy, uncomfortable with Little Calum's distress, and asked, "How about we bring you some of my favorite peanut butter candy?"

Mariana laughed. "When in doubt, bribery works. Plus, he needs more games."

Cal asked him, "What kind of games do you like to play?"

Immediately Little Calum gave him this long-winded explanation of the math game. Thankfully Cal recognized part of it. "You know what? I think I know what you mean, and there's another one that's kind of like that. Maybe I'll find you a couple to play."

At that, Sophia laughed. "*Uh-huh*, I see where this is going." She noticed how dissatisfied the young Calum was. "I don't know if you like computers, buddy," she suggested, "but I have some really smart games to play."

Immediately Calum raced over, climbing onto the chair beside her. Pulling the chair closer, she showed him some things.

Calum looked at Mariana. "I think it's time to run."

She chuckled quietly, as they slipped out.

"Where do you need to go?" Cal asked her, as he led the way back to the truck.

"I need to get clothing for Calum, clothing for me, and

some personal items." He raised an eyebrow. "Depending on how long we'll be here, monthly cycles won't quit, for one thing."

He nodded immediately. "Oh, got it. Sorry. So a drugstore."

"Yep, a drugstore, and we'll need food." He rolled his eyes at that one. "I should have taken a look at the kitchen," she mentioned. "I could cook now."

"Ask someone to send you photos. Maybe Terk would be better, leaving the women to continue their searches."

Wade had been quiet as he followed them outside, until now. He said to Calum, "Let me drive."

Cal looked at him in surprise. "Sure. Any particular reason?"

"It'll be easier for you to keep an eye out," he explained, "and I can drop you by the entry."

"Are we really expecting something?" Mariana asked the guys.

"If you don't expect it, you're not prepped for it," Wade replied immediately.

She sank into the back seat. "I feel like I should sit low, so that nobody can target my head from behind us."

"We've done that a time or two ourselves," Cal admitted, with a nod. "So it's not a bad idea."

After a few minutes, Wade added, letting them know, "Gage is driving behind us too."

At that, Mariana asked, "Is it that dangerous for us to be out here that we need two more people?"

"We've had too much trouble to take any chances," Cal said, with a gentle glance in her direction. "Don't take it personally or freak out. We're just trying to keep everybody safe."

She nodded slowly. "It's just a rude awakening to realize we can't even go shopping."

"Well, we've done plenty of shopping since we've been here—well at least the others have," Cal replied. "It's a necessary thing, since there's a lot of us to feed, but we also must ensure that we're not bringing anybody back home with us."

She nodded again. Just then came a buzz on her phone. "Oh, look at that," she said, as she stared down at the photo Tasha just sent. "Wow, there really is a full kitchen. It's perfect."

"Good," Cal replied. "It'll be easier to keep food in the place that way."

"She sent me more photos. I see big freezers and a commercial fridge of some kind. She's making sure everything is turned on."

"That's not a bad idea either," Cal noted. "And you're practically a chef anyway."

"Well, I don't know about being a chef," she admitted. "It seems like a long time ago that I cooked that much."

"It would be great to have something besides sandwiches," Wade said. "I just realized I don't know that much about you, Mariana. Have you been working all this time, or is the little guy your full-time job?"

"Both really," she replied. "I'm involved in the world of small business, so I can operate from home and yet be there with Little Calum. So, I am still working but only from home now."

"So, you're flexible then. I mean, if you don't go back."

"Yes," she replied.

"Will there be people looking for you?" Wade asked.

"We've kept a fairly low profile intentionally. I do have

family in London I'll need to contact eventually, but we're fine for now. It's pretty much been just Little Calum in my world." She reached over and squeezed Cal's shoulder, "And this one of course."

"And they're both definitely worth keeping," Wade added.

She laughed at that. "I'd like to think so. The jury is still out on what this one thinks though."

"No, it's not. Not at all," Cal argued.

"You guys just need time to sort it out," Wade suggested.

Wade was right, and she agreed with that, but time and privacy didn't appear to be something that they had available. By the time they got to town and started shopping, Cal said, "Listen. I didn't mean to suggest you have to do all the cooking for everyone. I'm certainly not telling you it's your job or anything like that."

"I didn't take it that way at all," she replied, "but obviously I need to contribute, and Lord knows Little Calum keeps me in the kitchen plenty anyway." There was a smile on her face, as she continued. "The little peanut butter monster can eat, and, besides that, if I'm cooking for three, I might as well cook for ten," she noted, "but do we have a budget for groceries?"

"Yeah, we'll be fine," Cal stated. "Let's get whatever we need. Now that we have some proper facilities, we'll stock up, but I'm warning you. Tasha eats a ton. We all do really, but she's pretty impressive."

"I've seen her in action," Mariana shared. "I did see her eat the other morning, and it looked like she could tank up pretty well."

"I think all of us can now. Terk would say that we're still

in the healing mode and that eating—even overeating—is a good sign," Wade added, catching up to them after parking the vehicle. "We're all pretty happy eaters, when we get a chance to. Especially when our energy is low."

She nodded. "Then grab another cart. We'll need it. Guess we should have done the clothing first," she fretted.

"We've been gone awhile already," Cal noted. "How long will you need for the clothes?"

She felt the pressure. "I won't need much time, as long as I can get to a store that's got what I need."

"We'll see that you do," he murmured, and, with that, they moved through the grocery store with precision, as she mentally checked off what would be needed.

By the time she had two large carts full, she whispered, "So this will cost a lot, like one thousand dollars plus here."

"We are stocking a new kitchen and with more than just one week's worth of food too. Plus, we're feeding a lot of people," he reminded her.

"You don't think anybody will notice us and think it suspicious?"

"Nope, I don't," he murmured. "Plenty of full carts surround us. What I do know is that, if you'll start cooking, I'll have to get myself on a diet."

She laughed. "You know I love cooking, but I've never done it every day, every meal, for this many people."

"Not to worry," Wade replied. "We'll all help. We'll take on some meals ourselves. We're a team. We'll distribute that duty so it doesn't fall to you for 365 days of breakfasts, lunches, and dinners. That wouldn't be fair."

Mariana nodded. "Thank you. As you know, the last few weeks, the last few months even, have been kind of disconcerting."

"You think?" Wade teased.

Then Cal laughed. "It'll work out. You'll see. Let's just get this done."

"Aren't we raising any eyebrows with all this?" she asked again.

"Maybe," he admitted, "but it's got to happen."

She winced. "We could have come late at night, I suppose."

"No way, that's when the really sketchy shoppers come out," Cal murmured, a smile in his voice. "If you think about it, just act natural."

"I don't have a problem *thinking* of acting natural. I have a problem *doing* it."

Cal, still chuckling, said, "I can see that." And now they were in line for the checkout.

"The problem will be," she noted, "I've surely forgotten stuff."

"It's fine. We can get more at another time. This will give us a hell of a start, and it will be a feast compared to what we've had to eat until now."

She agreed, but she also needed certain items on hand. She looked over the contents of both carts, reassuring herself that she had the basics. She'd already pretty well emptied the store, or at least that's how she felt.

As she left the cashier, she told the guys, "Now I'll need a department store. It doesn't have to be high-end. Anything is fine. I just need some clothes for me and for Little Calum."

"In that case," Wade mentioned, "a couple department stores are around the corner."

"Good," she said. "Let's start there."

"Can you get everything in one go?" Cal asked.

"I would hope so, but there's no way to know what they carry until I get there," she explained. "Luckily Little Calum's not a hard size to fit. He just needs something that he can be active in, running around the place. I'd like to get some comfortable shoes for him too."

"I guess the kidnappers just swept you up and took you away, didn't they?" Cal asked, with an odd tone, as if realizing it for the first time.

"If you thought it was safe," Mariana told him, "we could just go back to our place, and I could get a few more of his things, and that might make it a little easier for him."

Calum thought about it and looked over at Wade. "What do you think?"

Wade considered it, then said, "If it's not too far away, we could always have Tasha and the others set up satellite monitoring to keep an eye on us, and, with Gage already running background, it might not be the worst idea."

"So can we avoid the department store trip if we do that?" Cal asked her.

"Absolutely," she replied. "I don't have that much over there anyway, so it will be quick. Most of my things are still in Paris," she explained to Wade. "If I could at least access what's here nearby, that would make a huge difference, especially for Little Calum."

With that decision made, and the satellite monitoring in place, they immediately drove to the small apartment she had sublet.

"Whose apartment is this?" Cal asked.

"An old school friend's," she replied. When he looked at her in surprise, she shrugged cheerfully. "I do have friends. Remember?"

"It's not that," Cal noted. "I'm just ... Have you heard

from them?"

"Not recently, no," she stated. "I wasn't really expecting to either though. I rented it for six months."

"Okay," Cal said. "As long as they don't have any inkling that, with your absence here, there might be something wrong."

"No, I don't think so. I didn't tell them about what happened. I wasn't planning on telling anybody to be honest."

"And that's a good thing," Cal confirmed. "We don't really want any gossiping going on about what may or may not have happened."

"Not only that," she added, "I know they would just worry, and that won't help any of us."

"Nope, it sure won't," Cal murmured. "We'll get through this."

She shrugged. "They had the apartment sitting there and would be away anyway. I'd known they'd had it for a long time," she shared. "So, when I asked him about it, they were happy to rent it to me."

"Did it just happen to be empty?"

"It had been vacant for a couple months, while their plans were still up in the air, and they were waiting to see if they would need it themselves. Otherwise they were planning to rent it out. They still don't know the long-term answer to that, so letting me have it for six months solved a dilemma for them as well."

"Good enough," Cal said, "but obviously somebody knew where you were living."

She nodded. "If anybody did any real research on me, I'm sure my friends would have popped up." He hesitated as he watched her expression closely, and then she immediately swore. "Are you telling me that they're in danger?"

"Where do they live?"

"Right now? They've been in England for the last many months. Well, probably a couple years actually," she corrected. "So hopefully they aren't anybody that the bad guys are too bothered with."

"The fact that you rented the apartment probably triggered the whole kidnapping plan," Wade guessed.

"Right, *that* plan." She shook her head. "People need to get a life if all they have to do in their world is to hunt down innocent people."

"Don't forget that, for these guys, there is no such thing as innocent people." Cal shrugged.

She nodded slowly. "I can't imagine what that's like."

"It's shitty as hell," Cal stated quietly. "You start to look at everybody sideways, and then you begin to realize that people don't really have any values. That's the scary part, when they see you *not* as a human but as an object to further their means." He sounded weary, when he added, "It can get pretty ugly, pretty damn fast."

She didn't even want to think about it. "But would subletting show up in public records somewhere?"

"Good question," Wade noted.

Cal added, "If you're worried about it, we can always make discreet inquiries to see if the couple is okay."

She sighed. "I would just as soon not trigger any inquiries because that might put my friends back on somebody's radar."

Wade smiled. "Good thinking. It's always better if we don't bring more people into the mix."

"How did you pay the rent?" Cal asked.

"That might have triggered a search query. I did an etransfer from my bank to theirs."

"That would do it too." Cal nodded. "Particularly if the bad guys have access to your bank account."

"Well, that wouldn't be very nice to steal from me. It's not like I'm wealthy."

"And they would know that too," Wade murmured. Then he looked over at Cal and asked him, "Would that have been a trigger on your part?"

Cal looked at Wade and swore. "That's quite possible." He looked at Mariana, who seemed confused. "I sent you money."

She stared at him. "And you think they've been watching us for that long?" she asked. "Because that was a while ago."

"It would have just confirmed that we were still in touch and that you would still be decent hostage material."

"Jesus," she murmured. "You need to get some real friends."

"I have real friends"—he laughed—"and you've met a lot of them."

When she realized what he meant, she nodded. "I get that, but, you know, how about people who aren't trying to kill you?"

"These guys I work with and I'm friends with aren't trying to kill me. They're the good guys."

She smiled over at Wade. "How about you? Do you have friends?"

"Something better. ... I have the team," he said instantly. "When you're engaged in this kind of security and protection work that we do, it's not as if we can come home and tell just anybody what we did all day. It's pretty damn hard to have any other friends, outside of our circle of people we trust with our lives. The team knows what we do and understands how difficult it is on any 'outside' relationships to not be able to tell the truth, to keep the secrets that we keep. That segregates us pretty quickly. Then, when you add in our energy work, we are but a few. Therefore, not many people like us are out there."

"Right," she said, taking a deep breath. "I'm surprised so many of you have found partners."

"Are we all so unlikable?" Wade asked, laughing.

"No, not at all." She shook her head. "We're just back to that whole *they need to know what we do* thing …"

"Not just that but all of us working together helps with that part. We have a life with partners now, and it's different from others' relationships by a significant margin," Wade explained. "We met our matches but fought it initially, tried to avoid any permanent relationships, but it's now been kind of an awakening for some of us."

She nodded. "I get all that. I guess I'm just still surprised. Dating can be such an unsuccessful maze. It's so hard to find someone who's right for us. Yet you guys have extra elements to deal with. Seems like the odds would be against us, you know? Happy for you guys though. Don't get me wrong. I think the kind of work you guys do must be very lonely at times."

"That's putting it mildly. It can be a living hell sometimes," Wade murmured. "And it's something that we are aware of. It's just not something we can really do much about it."

She looked over at Cal. "Would you agree with that?"

He nodded. "You know how I feel about the work I do."

"I do know," she admitted, "just as you know how I felt about breaking up our family."

"I know. I was trying to keep you safe. But apparently the writing was already on the wall, since it appears these guys after us may have already had access to information about me and you and Little Calum. It was only a matter of time before somebody utilized that intel for their own gain."

"That's what I mean about the world you live in," she added, with a head shake. "It's not the easiest, that's for sure."

"No, it isn't," Cal agreed, "and you have to be very, very certain that you really understand and that you're up for that."

She looked at him with a frown. "Listen. If you're trying to chase me off again," she snapped, "don't bother."

He winced. "I'm not trying to chase you off. I just want to ensure that we're dealing with reality."

"My reality is that this right here is all we have to deal with, and I will." And, with that, she clammed up.

IT WASN'T THE easiest subject to bring up, but Cal also felt that she might be hiding something. Yet it wasn't the time or the place. As they pulled up to her apartment, Calum looked at it and said, "This is a nice little area."

"It was supposed to be," she noted, "but it's not looking that nice at the moment."

"You can't blame the neighborhood for the visitors," he replied.

"No, I know. I do know that," she murmured. "This just wasn't exactly the kind of vacation break I was hoping for."

And Cal knew exactly what she meant. They were still walking on tiptoes around each other, having broken the ice a few times, but, at the same time, a barrier still remained between them, and he knew it would take a while for more of that to thaw.

Wade was trying to stay out of the issues between them, but no way he could avoid the undercurrents. When they got out of the truck, he looked over at Calum intently. "I'll do a quick search around."

"Be careful."

"Got it."

Cal led the way up to the apartment. He saw no sign of any problems, and, with the satellite monitoring under Terk's watchful eye, Wade right here, and Gage nearby, Cal felt fairly safe in going in. "Let's go in and get what we need as fast as you can. Then we can return to the safety of headquarters."

She nodded, took a deep breath, then unlocked the door and stepped inside. She immediately cried out in horror.

He stepped in behind her. "Well, that answers that question."

She turned to look at him and asked, "What question?"

"If they found what they after," Cal said. "I wondered if they would have left this place as is or would have taken everything."

"You mean, besides doing this? I don't even know what they could have taken," she replied. "Is this just for show or because they were after something?" There was a surprising amount of destruction.

"Do you have anything for them to be after?" he asked.

She stared at him. "I don't know if that's just a random question or if you're accusing me of something," she told him, her voice sounding hurt, making him wince. "But either way, the answer to that is, I don't know because I

209

don't know what they're looking for."

"Hey, I'm not trying to accuse you of anything. Did you have any paperwork here or anything?"

She stared at him. "Nothing anybody would be interested in that I know of, but obviously we came here for another reason."

"Yes, I know," he agreed quietly, as he studied the room, taking a few photos. "Let's get what you need for now. We'll get this cleaned up after we figure things out."

"I have to get it cleaned up," she said. "Not only am I still paying rent on this, but my friends will be pissed if I leave it like this."

"We won't leave it like this," Cal promised. "Come on. Let's get what you need right now."

She led the way to the bedrooms. She noted some damage here, but less.

He nodded. "This is just for show. In case anybody looks into it, it appears to be a break-and-enter situation."

"God," she said, shaking her head, "how is this something for show?"

"Because they didn't trash the rest of it," he noted. "They could have done so much worse."

"I guess, but it's still disconcerting to see the kind of damage that they were okay to inflict for nothing."

"But that's what I mean," he said. "This was literally just for show, for anybody to see. So, if your body showed up in a canal down the road, it would look like a break-in that got carried away, maybe taking somebody away to have fun."

She swallowed hard at that.

"I'm really not trying to scare you but to warn you, to protect you, to inform you how these guys think. It's just another scenario."

At that, she quickly turned and headed to the closet. She pulled out a bag and said, "Help me pack up everything then."

Seeing all the clothes, he added, "Seems a washer and a dryer are in the new section of the warehouse too."

"Good, we'll need it. Particularly with a four-year-old." And, with that, they packed up as much as they could. Then she headed over to Little Calum's room.

"Did he stay here much?" Calum asked, as he looked around the room and frowned.

"No. He wanted to be in the room with me mostly."

"Right. It looks like this bedroom just held his stuff."

"I unpacked, and that's about it," she noted, with a half-hearted look around. "But we'll need every bit of his stuff that we can find. He grows fast as it is, so it'd be nice if we at least got a few months' use out of some of this."

He laughed. "We'll get more for him," he promised.

She glanced over at him, smiled, and said, "Even with the kidnapper and all this that followed, I don't regret coming here. You know that, right?"

He walked over, pulled her into his arms, and admitted, "I don't regret having you here either. I just don't want anything to happen to you two, and we're still not out of the woods."

"Something already happened to us," she noted, "and your son needs you more now than ever."

Hearing a buzz from his phone, he checked it quickly and said, "Let's go. Time to move."

"We've been here too long, I presume?"

"We have to keep our visits to a certain time frame, and we can't really afford to be tracked," he explained. "We have utilized this one to the max as it is."

"Are you saying that somebody could be following us?"

"No," he said. "I am saying that there is a standard procedure, and we have to follow it." Cal was trying hard not to let too much be known, yet he knew she needed to know more. "I do suspect that, when we opened that door, it triggered a notice for somebody to come here."

She stared at him and turned to run to the living room. "Let's go then. I really don't want to meet those guys again." He grabbed up their bags and led her safely downstairs, and, just as they were about to exit the front entrance, he stopped, then shook his head and pointed in the other direction. "Let's go around the back."

She stared at him. "Why?"

"I don't like it," he said in a quick tone.

She nodded slowly. "Okay. I'm good with that. It'd be nice if I had an idea why though."

"I told you. It's just instincts at this point."

She stopped and checked in with her own instincts. "Okay then, let's go," she murmured, "fast." He looked at her in surprise. She shrugged. "I can't say that I feel terribly secure about being here, and I'd like to leave." As soon as they hit the back parking lot, a shout came from the left.

Out of habit, he dropped to the ground, with her in his arms, and rolled.

Not easy or smooth while their bags went flying and when a hard *oomph* hit his chest. When a whistle came through, he pulled her up into a crouch behind a nearby vehicle.

"What the hell was that?" she asked, holding her arm.

He glanced at her, concern in his eyes. "Are you okay?"

"Yes, yes. … I'm fine." Obviously she was rattled but he was holding her, and that was worth everything.

He replied, "That was a warning from Wade."

"Great. So you're correct?"

"It looks like it," he said, his tone grim. "It also means they're closer than we expected."

"Physically located closer?" she asked.

He nodded. "Yeah, otherwise they wouldn't have made it here this fast. I had hoped we had enough time to get out, but it doesn't look like it."

"Well, maybe this is the better way after all," she murmured. "Can we make this all come to a head and call it quits today?" He looked over at her, and she shrugged. "I really don't want to worry about being followed every time I'm out."

"It'll be that way until we get to the bottom of the original attack," he stated.

"I know, and you're warning me that this is just the way it is," she murmured. "I get it. I really do, but, if this will be crunch time, let's at least have it be a successful crunch time. I've got groceries to get in the fridge, so hurry it up."

He looked at her, as he let out a soft bark of laughter. "I wish you were in that vehicle right now."

She thought about it and asked him, "Should I make a run for it? I can go there."

He shook his head. "Not alone. Not now."

She nodded. "Well then, it's up to you to fix this, so go on." And she gave him a gentle push. He glared at her, and she shrugged vehemently. "You're not staying here and worrying about me, while I'm sitting here worrying about stuff to go in the freezer," she explained, with half a smile.

He just rolled his eyes at that. "I highly doubt that's what's on your mind."

"Oh, I don't know. You might be surprised. What I do

need is to get back to Little Calum."

"That's a given," he said. Still he hesitated, but she needed him to get into the moment.

"Stop overthinking it, and just go do your thing. If you see the bad guys, then you do what you need to do. If we can get me to the vehicle and if that's a safe place for me to hide, I'll stay there."

"I'm not sure if it is or not," he admitted, "because I don't know what the problem is." Just then his phone buzzed. He pulled it out. "What's going on, Terk?"

"You've got visitors."

"Yeah, we figured that much out," he said, "but what I don't know is where they are, how many, or what they're after."

"You can pretty well guarantee it'll be you who they want, and she'll be taken as collateral damage," he replied in his caustic tonal voice. "We've got you on satellite. Wade drove the truck around to the back, if you can get there," he noted. "That would at least give you some cover."

"Where is Wade now?"

"He's on the hunt."

"Well shit, I want to go on the hunt too."

"I don't think that's a good idea right now."

As he looked over at Mariana at his side, he nodded. "No, I need to get her safely out of here."

"I told you," she said. "Point me in the direction of the truck, and I'll make it myself."

But he wasn't listening. No way she would make it safely to the truck from here. "Do we have snipers again?" Cal asked Terk.

"I'm not sure that you do," Terk replied, "but we haven't found any on satellite."

"Good God, Mariana, I thought he shot you. Let me help you up. We need to leave now."

"No, we need this to be over with. So you need to do whatever you need to do to bring this to a conclusion."

Just then more gunshots burst out on the other side of the parking lot.

"Hopefully," Cal said, "that just finished it."

Then came a shout in their direction.

"I need to check it out." He stopped to take a photo of his dead guy.

"I'm coming too," she replied.

"No way in hell ..."

"I'm not staying here alone," she snapped.

So together they walked over carefully to Wade, standing over another man, while stepping on the gun beside him, also taking a photo of his guy.

"Is he dead?" she asked.

"Yeah, and it's getting pretty hard to talk to anybody when they keep wiping them out," Wade noted, glaring at the dead guy.

"Agreed. Mine is dead too," Cal confirmed.

"Yours is understandable," Wade stated. "He was trying to shoot her. In my case, I was really hoping I could talk him down, and we could keep him alive, at least long enough to get some information. Yet I don't think anybody will come to us alive. I didn't shoot him though," he shared. "The damn drones did."

"And it didn't shoot you at the same time?" Cal asked.

Wade shook his head. "No, but then again"—he pointed to the ground a short distance away—"I didn't give it a chance." There, on the parking lot, was the drone.

"Well, hell," Calum said. "That might be good, or it

might not, depending on if Tasha and the others can do anything with it."

"I hope so," Wade added, "but, either way, this chapter is closed."

Cal looked over at Mariana. "What's wrong? You're looking at our DB funny."

"I recognize him," she said quietly. "I think he was one of the workmen on the day I moved into the apartment. He asked if he could check ... something. Let me think. Yeah, he said that he'd heard I was moving in and that he needed to check on the furnace to make sure everything was functioning."

"So you let him in?" Calum asked.

She nodded slowly. "I did."

"And, in that moment," he said, "he confirmed that you were the person they were looking for, how many of you there were, and, in the end, the bad guys took this inform-ant's life too."

She shook her head. "My God, they must really want you guys badly."

"You have no idea," Calum said, holding her tight, "but remember. This is not your fault. They already knew about our presence here, or he wouldn't have been hanging around, waiting for us to show up somewhere. So they would have confirmed it was us soon enough."

She nodded slowly. "I hear you. I see it even, but some-how it still doesn't seem real."

"None of it is for real," he noted. "It's temporary, and it will pass. The good news is that, this time, Little Calum isn't involved."

"No, you're right. That is the good news." She looked over at Wade, then back to Cal. "Can we go back now?"

Cal held her close and whispered, "Yes." He then turned and looked at Wade, with one eyebrow raised.

Wade nodded. "I'm waiting for Terk."

"Terk or Merk?" Cal asked.

"Probably both of them, now that we have two more dead bodies," Wade guessed. "Merk will stop taking our calls soon."

Cal smiled. "Never. We're ridding the world of guys who could come after him next. Levi and Ice are no doubt planning contingencies in case that should happen."

"Jesus. I wonder how far-reaching this will be?" Wade asked.

"I hope not that far," Cal noted. "They've been good friends, and, if anything happens to their team, you know we'll go back and hunt down whoever's involved."

"You know for a fact that Terk is resilient. He'll go deal with whatever hell is going on with Celia too."

"Yeah, that whole thing is bound to be tearing him apart, and he's stuck over here, dealing with this."

"Yeah, I haven't heard an update in a while, but I'll ask when he gets here."

"You know what? I get that the whole thing is a struggle, but she can't stay in a coma forever."

"I still can't believe somebody used her like that. She's an innocent victim in this whole mess."

"Do we know that for sure?" Cal asked Wade.

Wade frowned, and his gaze was hard. "I guess we don't, but I sure would like to think so."

"You and me both," Cal replied, "and I sure would like to see Terk catch a break for once. Everything has been a roller coaster for him for a very long time."

"Yeah, I get it," Wade noted. "You guys go. I'll hitch a

ride back with Gage. We'll take care of this. Make sure you get these photos to Tasha, to see if we can get them ID'd and track them any further."

"We will," he stated, "and hopefully it'll lead to the next piece of the puzzle. We just don't know what that'll be." And, with that, he bundled Mariana back up into the now empty truck with their bags of clothing and headed home. As soon as they returned to headquarters, he drove around to the farthest side of this row of warehouses, so that there was no direct connection to their main section, plus made it easier for unloading their haul. Then he led her through the building to the area where the commercial kitchen was.

She stopped and stared all around. "You know what? This is almost worth being here for." She rubbed her hands together.

"You go grab Little Calum," he said, "and I'll start putting away this food."

She nodded. "I'll do that." She turned but froze. Looking over her shoulder, she asked, "Where do I go?"

He pointed her to a doorway. "Go through there. It leads down one level to a basement area. Stay in the main hallway. At the third doorway, go up one floor, and you should be in our usual part of the warehouse. Text me if you need help."

She hoped she had appeared at least somewhat calm and contained. She didn't want it to look like she couldn't handle things, though it was pretty damn hard. She wanted to scream and rant and rave at the world for the scenario she had just been put through.

But, more than that, she wanted to hug somebody and to show gratitude for the fact that they were safe and sound and that more of these bad men were out of the picture. And

Cal was right. Their son hadn't seen anything this time, and hopefully time would help ease back some of his nightmares too.

She didn't know about hers, but hopefully, when she finally had a chance to crash, the events of the day would be something she could handle by crying it out. She found Little Calum still sitting on an office chair, adjusted perfectly for his small body, with a computer game playing on the screen. She watched him, as he thoroughly enjoyed whatever it was. He loved the game that he was playing, and she liked him that way, so happy and safe. "How is he?"

Sophia looked up and smiled at her. "He's doing just fine. If you need a few minutes to regroup, then go."

Mariana nodded and winced. "I do actually. Are you okay with that?"

She waved her away. "Don't worry about him. He's content."

Mariana headed to her bedroom, sat down on the side of the bed, and took several deep breaths. She needed to somehow get a grip on all this. She'd been holding off any breakdown, so it didn't look like she was completely overwhelmed, but the reality was, a man had tried to kill her, and she had seen him die right in front of her. She had come very close to death again. Twice in about thirty minutes.

She sat here and buried her face in her hands for a long moment, feeling her shoulders tremble.

When the door opened, she was desperate to try to regain some measure of control, but she was picked up and settled on Cal's lap, his arms wrapped tightly around her. He held her close. "I didn't think you'd handle much more. Just cry it out now, and then Little Calum won't know."

She lifted a tear-stained face to him. "That's what I was

trying to do. Somehow it's not that easy."

"It'll take time," he replied quietly. "This is why I was so desperate to keep you out of my world."

She nodded. "I understand it more now, but guess what? It didn't work."

He leaned over, tilted her head up, and gave her a gentle kiss on the cheek. "I'm worried that this isn't a life you want to lead."

"No, maybe it isn't, but I do want to have a life with you." She needed to let it all out. "So, if this is what our options are," she said, with a shrug, "I'll just have to get used to it."

He added, "It'll never be like this again."

She lifted a finger and placed it against his lips. "You mean, you *hope* it won't be." There needed to be understanding between them, and she did not need hollow words. "There's no way to know for sure what'll go down when there will always be crazies out there, trying to take you out."

"They don't even know about me," he said, with half a smile. "This is the first time we've ever personally come under attack, unless we were on a mission."

"Well, that's good news," she replied, smiling. "I'd hate to think that everybody hated you all the time."

He burst out laughing and gave her a gentle kiss. "Never."

As she looked up at him, she asked, "What are we doing? We need to clear the air."

"Sure, but we've hardly had a chance for that kind of conversation."

"Yes and no," she murmured.

"We're avoiding it. That's because we're afraid of what each other will say." They were in sync, even completing each other's sentences.

"I don't want to be afraid anymore," she admitted, her eyes huge. "Being afraid to me will now be related to getting shot or having to deal with assholes like that. I really don't want any of that to be part of my future."

"I got it," he murmured. "And I agree. So what is it you want to do?"

"What do I want to do?" she repeated. "I want to know that there is a you with me and that we're good and that this will be a good thing for us."

"As far as I'm concerned, it's the best thing for us," he murmured.

"Are you sure? You haven't really said anything before now."

"You mean like, *I love you*, or that I was just waiting for a chance to get you back into my life and that I am angry that I missed out on so much of Little Calum's childhood already and that I would have done anything to not put you two through what we just did?"

She nodded. "That's a good start," she whispered, looping her arms around his neck, "but it might take a little more convincing."

He smiled and held her close. "We have more time now, and together we can figure this out."

"As long as you stop trying to send me away," she stated. "I know why you did it, but we're not discussing that anymore. It's over, and I need to know that what we have now will remain so."

"I have no problem with that," he admitted. "I might worry more, and I might be less complacent about it than some of them," he noted, trying really hard, "but I promise I'll work on it."

She smiled. "Just make sure that you keep coming back to us," she added, "and then it'll be fine."

He nodded. "I'll do my best to do that. I'll have to get used to having a family around," he admitted. "It's not something I've ever had any chance to adapt to."

"Nope, but you will. There's really not a whole lot of choice." He burst out laughing, and she groaned. "See? You're already so much better off."

He smiled at her broadly. "I think you're quite right about that. I probably am way better off. I just need to make sure that you guys are too."

She pulled his head down toward her and said, "Not a problem. I already know that you are better off."

"And what about Little Calum?" he murmured.

"We already know how much he adores you—so as long as you're okay with being number one in his life," she said, laughing.

"I'll never be number one," he argued, "but I'm totally okay to be number two." And, with that, he lowered his head and kissed her, and almost too fast a heat built between them.

"Oh, that's dangerous," she murmured.

"It is," he agreed. "It's also addictive." He murmured in her ear, "I've missed you so much."

With tears in her eyes, she nodded. "I've missed you too."

He got up and said, "When I came in, Calum was playing computer games."

She nodded. He locked the door, as she stared at him and giggled. "You think that'll stop your son?"

"Well, at least slow him down long enough that we can maybe recover for a minute," he said. "This is our future life, isn't it? Locking doors and trying to find the time?"

"Yep," she agreed. "He's a very lively little boy, and you're not fooling him for long."

"Don't intend to fool him at all. Can we have the sex talk with him early?" he asked, grinning, and her eyes got wider. "Somewhere along the line, we must have some time for us too." He slowly lowered her onto the bed. "So, how about now?"

"Hey, now works just fine," she whispered. "We've got at least five minutes."

He rolled his eyes at that and chuckled. "Challenge accepted."

She burst out laughing and stripped off her clothes as fast as she could. When he realized what she was up to, he matched her, piece for piece.

By the time they fell back onto the bed, both of them without clothing, he wrapped her up in his arms. "I remember this, just that freedom, … that joy of being with you."

She gently placed her finger on his lips and whispered, "More action, less talk." He burst out laughing yet again, and she remembered the joy of hearing his voice and hearing that laughter, which sounded a bit rusty.

When he lowered his head and took her lips with that possessiveness which she remembered from the last time, she succumbed almost instantly. By the time he settled between her thighs, she was already panting and sweating on the bed. "Dear God," she said. "How is it even possible to feel like this and survive?"

"It's called being alive," he replied simply, as he slid into the heart of her.

She moaned, shuffling underneath him. "I forgot," she murmured, "but how could a person forget such a thing?"

"Because to remember all the good times is far too hard," he admitted. "I think we forget out of self-preservation."

"Well, enough of that," she said, as she lifted her hips up against him. "This isn't something that we do without anymore," she murmured. "As long as our hearts are there, we can work on everything else."

"Ditto," he murmured. And slowly he started to move. When she came apart in his arms, she knew she'd come home. Finally safe and sound. She knew that, if ever anybody would work hard at keeping her and Little Calum safe, it was this man, who held their hearts in his hand.

She murmured, "We have to unlock the door for him, but I really don't want to get back up."

"Take a break," he said. "If you want to just stay here, I'm all for it. I need to get back out there, but you don't."

She nodded, then yawned and said, "Honest to God, I could just stay here. I'm not tired, but, at the same time, I am. I want a shower, clean clothes, but that takes energy. … Does that make any sense?"

"Do what you have to do." He reached over and kissed her and pulled a blanket over her and said, "I'll send Little Calum in to curl up in bed with you."

"Okay, or you can give him a little bit longer with his game," she murmured, "if he's happy and not any trouble for the others. By the way, I think I hear telepathically, I kinda stayed in touch that way."

He started. Smiled. "Maybe it's something I can develop more now that we're together. But I'd have done anything to stay in contact." She yawned. "I don't know what time it is, but maybe I'll be fine after a nap."

"Doesn't matter what time it is," he whispered, as she closed her eyes.

CAL GOT UP quickly and pulled on his clothes, realizing that she'd once again fallen asleep immediately, much like the child out in the other room. He was still buzzing from that tidbit bombshell she'd dropped. It made sense in a way. And he couldn't be happier. With any luck, they'd be able to speak telepathically after being together again for a while too. It seemed a bit like the wild, wild west in terms of abilities now.

She'd always been like that, something he'd always found to be precious. He was almost jealous because she had that capacity to just disconnect from the world around her. But she would need it, if she would be a part of his world. It would be a saving grace if she would stay.

And he really wanted her to stay. He just needed to keep her safe. Now that they had taken out everybody on the ground involved in her kidnapping, it was hard not to believe that they could actually do this *living together* option.

Dressed, he unlocked the door and stepped out to check on Little Calum first. But he was still happily slamming away on the keyboard. Cal smiled. "You're quite the little gamer, aren't you?"

"It's fun, Daddy."

He laughed, then looked at the others and mouthed *thank you*. They just smiled and nodded. "Your mom is having a nap," Cal told his son.

"Good, she's tired. I'm not tired. I get to stay up late."

"Do you now?" he asked, watching with amusement as his son correctly answered several math questions to get another blast at some monster in their midst. "What makes you think I'll believe that?"

"Because you love me," he said instantly.

Cal burst out laughing. "Oh, I love you, indeed, but I'm pretty certain it's your bedtime." At that, Little Calum's shoulders sagged, as he looked over at Sophia. "May I play tomorrow?" he asked in his most polite and innocent way, which was a clear ploy to get in the door.

"You sure can," she told him, "if it's okay with your parents and all." His face lit up like a Christmas tree. "We can talk about it in the morning and set you back up again."

"Thank you," he said, beaming at her, before he scuttled off. "Daddy, ... you have to watch me brush my teeth."

Not exactly sure what the routine was, Cal let his son show him. In no time he had tucked him in beside his mother, who was sound asleep, and Cal gave his son a good night kiss.

As he walked back into the control room, he sidestepped over to the coffeepot and poured himself a cup. Then he leaned against the wall and turned to look at the two women.

"Is she doing okay?" Tasha asked worriedly.

"She is, but it was tough. I mean, the guy died right in front of her, after trying to take her out, twice."

"But you also saved her, so that would have gone a long way to making her feel better," Sophia added.

He smiled, then nodded. "I hope so."

Just then Terk came in, an odd look on his face.

"What's the matter?" Cal asked.

Terk shook his head. "I just got an SOS call," he murmured.

"From whom?"

"Rick."

Everybody bolted to their feet. "Rick?" Tasha repeated. "Is he awake?"

"No," Terk said. "That's the problem. The SOS call is literally from his consciousness."

"Jesus," Calum replied. "What do you want us to do with that? If he isn't even awake, he could still be caught up in a nightmare."

"I know," Terk agreed. "I'll go see him."

"Do you know where he is?" Tasha asked.

Terk looked over and smiled at them all. "Of course. I was the one who arranged the locations."

"You can't go alone," Tasha said, worriedly.

"I'm not going to." He looked over at Calum. "Are you up for it?"

"Absolutely." Then he looked at the others, with a torn expression. "Let my family know that I'll be back—if not later tonight, at least before morning."

They nodded.

Cal looked at Terk. "Come on. I'm ready." And together, they raced outside.

"Are you sure it was him?" Calum asked.

"Of course I'm sure it was him," Terk stated briskly, "but what I didn't share was that he wasn't alone."

"Somebody else? … Who?" Cal asked.

"I'm definitely getting female readings."

They stopped near the vehicle, and Cal hopped into the driver's seat. "And when you say, female …"

"I don't think that's what the call for help is about," Terk explained, "but I just know that someone's there."

"Well, I guess we better go find out. Have you got nurses on the clock?"

"I do, indeed," he said, with a sigh. "And I suspect that's what I'm hearing."

"And is that a problem?"

"Not necessarily, unless ..." And Terk stopped, then looking at Cal and added, "Unless we're dealing with another betrayal."

"Oh, God," Calum said. "Give me the address."

EPILOGUE

RICK HUCKLEBEE STRUGGLED with his consciousness. Something was there. Something was eating at him, and he could feel it. *Danger everywhere.*

Somebody was trying to hold him down, and he cried out for help again and again, but there just didn't seem to be any answer. And suddenly there was Terk.

"I'm here, Rick. Calm down. I'm right here."

Rick took several gasping breaths. "Dear God, what the hell is going on?"

"The team was attacked," Terk replied quietly. "You need to rest and recover."

"Am I alive?"

"You are." Then Terk hesitated. "You are alive but still unconscious."

At that, Rick stared at the man in front of him. "But I can see you."

"I know you can. You were always good at that."

"Says you," he murmured. "What do you mean, the team was attacked?"

"You heard me. The team, everyone, was attacked, and we have all been struggling to get back to normal. You've been in a coma, part of it self-induced, part of it medically induced, so you could heal. Now we need to carefully bring you into consciousness, but you're fighting everything we're doing."

"Of course I'm fighting everything," he murmured. "I don't understand how any of this could happen."

"None of us do," Terk noted. "The bottom line is, you're alive, and you'll be with Cara."

"I've felt somebody around me these last few days," he confirmed, "but the feelings have been getting stronger and stronger."

"Well, definitely people are around you," Terk replied. "Have you felt any dangerous energy?"

"Yes, that's what I'm trying to tell you." He gripped Terk's hand. "I don't know what it is or who it is, but, every time I try to move, I can't. It's like being locked up in a prison."

"I know," Terk murmured. "Take it easy, and I'll help bring you back, as soon as it is safe for you. Just give me a little bit of time."

"A little bit of time?" he repeated. "How much? I need out of here."

"And you're coming out," he stated firmly. "You've trusted me up until now. Don't lose that faith."

"No, no, … of course not," Rick said, taking several calming breaths. "Just get me up now," he snapped in a hard tone.

At that, Terk smiled and said, "Open your eyes."

Slowly Rick opened his eyes to see Terk standing there, with Calum beside him. Rick stared at them several moments, waiting for his consciousness to slowly filter in. "Jesus. Am I ever glad to see you."

Cal reached out, obviously caught up in emotions, and gripped his hand. "The feeling is mutual, man," Cal said. "I'm so damn glad to see that you're awake."

"What the hell happened?" Rick murmured. But his voice was a croak, sounding nothing like it was supposed to. He tried again. "What happened?"

"Too much," Terk replied. "At least too much to explain all at once. Listen. We need you to recover slowly and to get back on your feet."

"There's no such thing as recover slowly in my world," Rick argued. "You know that."

"You might find things are a little different now," Terk noted, searching him.

Rick stared at him. "In what way?"

"You may have lost a few abilities," he stated. "Yet you may have gained something. I don't know."

Just then a voice that he knew stepped forward and said, "I really think this is a bad idea."

"You might," Terk agreed, "but he's awake, so there's not a whole lot we'll do about it now."

Rick stared at the woman beside him. "It's been you," he said in an almost surly tone, frowning at her. "You're the one who's been looking after me."

She nodded. "I have. Terk hired me."

"I feel like—" And he stopped, shaking his head. "I know it sounds stupid, but I feel like she's involved."

At that, Terk stiffened. "Involved in what?"

"I don't know," Rick replied, studying her.

Terk turned to look at her. "Have you had any other visitors?"

She shook her head. "No, I told you that. We've also got cameras all over the place," she added in a calm tone. "We also know that, when they come out of a coma, they're very disoriented." She glared at Rick. "So I don't know what you mean by *involved*, but I'm certainly not involved in anything untoward," she stated. "I've been here for the last several weeks, looking after you."

Terk reached out a hand and gently patted hers. "And it's appreciated. Rick will need to stay here for a few more days at least, in order to get his head together."

"Like hell." Rick drew back the blankets and tried to sit up. And blinked. He was in a room, white, with no carpet, some wood flooring, but he was alone. The room was empty. He turned his head around and stared. "Hello," he cried out, and almost instantly a door opened. And that same woman walked in, took one look at him, and raced forward. "Lie down," she barked. "Take it easy."

He stared at her in shock. "Where's Terk?" he asked. "I was just talking to him."

She stared at him. "Nobody is here but you and me," she murmured. And then she helped him lie back down again. "Please relax. You've just come out of a coma, and you need to rest." She immediately slapped on a blood pressure cuff and started going over his vitals.

Nothing she did could change the shock in his head. He wasn't alone; he hadn't been alone. Everyone, including her, had been here.

So what the hell just happened?

This concludes Book 4 of Terkel's Team: Calum's Contact.

Read about Rick's Road: Terkel's Team, Book 5

Terkel's Team: Rick's Road (Book #5)

Welcome to a brand-new series from *USA Today* best-selling author Dale Mayer, where dark-ops SEALs have special senses and skills, needed to solve intrigue, betrayal, and ... murder. A series with all the elements you've come to love, plus so much more, ... including psychics!

Stubborn was something Rick had been called a lot. *Independent. A loner.* All true but, once a powerful healer connects to bring him back from the brink of death, Rick is in danger of losing that control and that privacy he so values.

Cara understands Rick's need to be alone, but it's not likely possible any longer, and that isn't something she's ready to tell him. That and the value of the connection they now share is something he has to find out for himself.

And the sooner, the better, as the attacks on the team continue, their temporary headquarters under surveillance, and their much-vaulted skills nowhere in sight ...

Find Book 5 here!
To find out more visit Dale Mayer's website.
http://smarturl.it/DMSTTRick

Magnus: Shadow Recon (Book #1)

Deep in the permafrost of the Arctic, a joint task force, comprised of over one dozen countries, comes together to level up their winter skills. A mix of personalities, nationalities, and egos bring out the best—and the worst—as these globally elite men and women work and play together. They rub elbows with hardy locals and a group of scientists gathered close by …

One fatality is almost expected with this training. A second is tough but not a surprise. However, when a third goes missing? It's hard to not be suspicious. When the missing man is connected to one of the elite Maverick team members and is a special friend of Lieutenant Commander Mason Callister? All hell breaks loose ...

LIEUTENANT COMMANDER MASON Callister walked into the private office and stood in front of retired Navy Commander Doran Magellan.

"Mason, good to see you."

Yet the dry tone of voice, and the scowl pinching the silver-haired man, all belied his words. Mason had known Doran for over a decade, and their friendship had only grown over time.

Mason waited, as he watched the other man try to work the new tech phone system on his desk. With his hand circling the air above the black box, he appeared to hit buttons randomly.

Mason held back his amusement but to no avail.

"Why can't a phone be a phone anymore?" the commander snapped, as his glare shifted from Mason to the box and back.

Asking the commander if he needed help wouldn't make the older man feel any better, but sitting here and watching as he indiscriminately punched buttons was a struggle. "Is Helen away?" Mason asked.

"Yes, damn it. She's at lunch, and I need her to be at lunch." The commander's piercing gaze pinned Mason in place. "No one is to know you're here."

Solemn, Mason nodded. "Understood."

"Doran? Is that you?" A crotchety voice slammed into the room through the phone's speakers. "Get away from that damn phone. You keep clicking buttons in my ear. Get

239

Helen in there to do this."

"No, she can't be here for this."

Silence came first, then a huge groan. "Damn it. Then you should have connected me last, so I don't have to sit here and listen to you fumbling around."

"Go pour yourself a damn drink then," Doran barked. "I'm working on the others."

A snort was his only response.

Mason bit the inside of his lip, as he really tried to hold back his grin. The retired commander had been hell on wheels while on active duty, and, even now, the retired part of his life seemed to be more of a euphemism than anything.

"Damn things ..."

Mason looked around the dark mahogany office and the walls filled with photos, awards, medals. A life of purpose, accomplishment. And all of that had only piqued his interest during the initial call he'd received, telling him to be here at this time.

"Ah, got it."

Mason's eyebrows barely twitched, as the commander gave him a feral grin. "I'd rather lead a warship into battle than deal with some of today's technology."

As he was one of only a few commanders who'd been in a position to do such a thing, it said much about his capabilities.

And much about current technology.

The commander leaned back in his massive chair and motioned to the cart beside Mason. "Pour three cups."

Interesting. Mason walked a couple steps across the rich tapestry-style carpet and lifted the silver service to pour coffee into three very down-to-earth-looking mugs.

"Black for me."

Mason picked up two cups and walked one over to Doran.

"Thanks." He leaned forward and snapped into the phone, "Everyone here?"

Multiple voices responded.

Curiouser and curiouser. Mason recognized several of the voices. Other relics of an era gone by. Although not a one would like to hear that, and, in good faith, it wasn't fair. Mason had thought each of these men were retired, had relinquished power. Yet, as he studied Doran in front of him, Mason had to wonder if any of them actually had passed the baton or if they'd only slid into the shadows. Was this planned with the government's authority? Or were these retirees a shadow group to the government?

The tangible sense of power and control oozed from Doran's words, tone, stature—his very pores. This man might be heading into his sunset years—based on a simple calculation of chronological years spent on the planet—but he was a long way from being out of the action.

"Mason ..." Doran began.

"Sir?"

"We've got a problem."

Mason narrowed his gaze and waited.

Doran's glare was hard, steely hard, with an icy glint. "Do you know the Mavericks?"

Mason's eyebrows shot up. The black ops division was one of those well-kept secrets, so, therefore, everyone knew about it. He gave a decisive nod. "I do."

"And you're involved in the logistics behind the ICE training program in the Arctic, are you not?"

"I am." Now where was the commander going with this?

"Do you know another SEAL by the name of Mountain

Rode? He's been working for the black ops Mavericks." At his own words, the commander shook his head. "What the hell was his mother thinking when she gave him that moniker?"

"She wasn't thinking anything," said the man with a hard voice from behind Mason.

He stiffened slightly, then relaxed as he recognized that voice too.

"She died giving birth to me. And my full legal name is Mountain Bear Rode. It was my father's doing."

The commander glared at the new arrival. "Did I say you could come in?"

"Yes." Mountain's voice was firm, yet a definitive note of affection filled his tone.

That emotion told Mason so much.

The commander harrumphed, then cleared his throat. "Mason, we're picking up a significant amount of chatter over that ICE training. Most of it good. Some of it the usual caterwauling we've come to expect every time we participate in a joint training mission. This one is set to run for six months, then to reassess."

Mason already knew this. But he waited for the commander to get around to why Mason was here, and, more important, what any of this had to do with the mountain of a man who now towered beside him.

The commander shifted his gaze to Mountain, but he remained silent.

Mason noted Mountain was not only physically big but damn imposing and severely pissed, seemingly barely holding back the forces within. His body language seemed to yell, *And the world will fix this, or I'll find the reason why.*

For a moment Mason felt sorry for the world.

Finally a voice spoke through the phone. "Mason, this is

Alpha here. I run the Mavericks. We've got a problem with that ICE training center. Mountain, tell him."

Mason shifted to include Mountain in his field of vision. Mason wished the other men on the conference call were in the room too. It was one thing to deal with men you knew and could take the measure of; it was another when they were silent shadows in the background.

"My brother is one of the men who reported for the Artic training three weeks ago."

"Tergan Rode?" Mason confirmed. "I'm the one who arranged for him to go up there. He's a great kid."

A glimmer of a smile cracked Mountain's stony features. He nodded. "Indeed. A bright light in my often dark world. He's a dozen years younger than me, just passed his BUD/s training this spring, and raring to go. Until his raring to go then got up and went."

Oh, shit. Mason's gaze zinged to the commander, who had kicked up his feet to rest atop the big desk. Stocking feet. With Mickey Mouse images dancing on them. Sidetracked, Mason struggled to pull his attention back to Mountain. "Meaning?"

"He's disappeared." Mountain let out a harsh breath, as if just saying that out loud, and maybe to the right people, could allow him to relax—at least a little.

The commander spoke up. "We need your help, Mason. You're uniquely qualified for this problem."

It didn't sound like he was qualified in any way for anything he'd heard so far. "Clarify." His spoken word simplicity itself, but the tone behind it said he wanted the cards on the table … now.

Mountain spoke up. "He's the third incident."

Mason's gaze narrowed, as the reports from the training camp rolled through his mind. "One was Russian. One was from the German SEAL team. Both were deemed accidental deaths."

"No, they weren't."

There it was. The root of the problem in black-and-white. He studied Mountain, aiming for neutrality. "Do you have evidence?"

"My brother did."

"Ah, hell."

Mountain gave a clipped nod. "I'm going to find him."

"Of that I have no doubt," Mason said quietly. "Do you have a copy of the evidence he collected?"

"I have some of it." Mountain held out a USB key. "This is your copy. Top secret."

"We don't have to remind you, Mason, that lives are at stake," Doran added. "Nor do we need another international incident. Consider also that a group of scientists, studying global warming, is close by, and not too far away is a village home to a few hardy locals."

Mason accepted the key, turned to the commander, and asked, "Do we know if this is internal or enemy warfare?"

"We don't know at this point," Alpha replied through the phone. "Mountain will lead Shadow Recon. His mission is twofold. One, find out what's behind these so-called accidents and put a stop to it by any means necessary. Two, locate his brother, hopefully alive."

"And where do I come in?" Mason asked.

"We want you to pull together a special team. The members of Shadow Recon will report to both you and Mountain, just in case."

That was clear enough.

"You'll stay stateside but in constant communication with Mountain—with the caveat that, if necessary, you're on the next flight out."

"What about bringing in other members from the Mavericks?" Mason suggested.

Alpha took this question too, his response coming through via Speakerphone. "We don't have the numbers. The budget for our division has been cut. So we called the commander to pull some strings."

That was Doran's cue to explain further. "Mountain has fought hard to get me on board with this plan, and I'm here now. The navy has a special budget for Shadow Recon and will take care of Mountain and you, Mason, and the team you provide."

"Skills needed?"

"Everything," Mountain said, his voice harsh. "But the biggest is these men need to operate in the shadows, mostly alone, without a team beside them. Too many new arrivals will alert the enemy. If we make any changes to the training program, it will raise alarms. We'll move the men in one or two at a time on the same rotation that the trainees are running right now."

"And when we get to the bottom of this?" Mason looked from the commander back to Mountain.

"Then the training can resume as usual," Doran stated.

Mason immediately churned through the names already popping up in his mind. How much could he tell his men? Obviously not much. Hell, he didn't know much himself. How much time did he have? "Timeline?"

The commander's final word told him of the urgency.

"Yesterday."

Find Magnus here!

To find out more visit Dale Mayer's website.

smarturl.it/DMSSRMagnus

Author's Note

Thank you for reading Calum's Contact: Terkel's Team, Book 4! If you enjoyed the book, please take a moment and leave a short review.

Dear reader,

I love to hear from readers, and you can contact me at my website: www.dalemayer.com or at my Facebook author page. To be informed of new releases and special offers, sign up for my newsletter or follow me on BookBub. And if you are interested in joining Dale Mayer's Reader Group, here is the Facebook sign up page.
https://smarturl.it/DaleMayerFBGroup

Cheers,
Dale Mayer

Get THREE Free Books Now!

Have you met the SEALS of Honor?

SEALs of Honor Books 1, 2, and 3. Follow the stories of brave, badass warriors who serve their country with honor and love their women to the limits of life and death.

Read Mason, Hawk, and Dane right now for FREE.

Go here and tell me where to send them!
http://smarturl.it/EthanBofB

About the Author

Dale Mayer is a *USA Today* best-selling author, best known for her SEALs military romances, her Psychic Visions series, and her Lovely Lethal Garden cozy series. Her contemporary romances are raw and full of passion and emotion (Broken But ... Mending, Hathaway House series). Her thrillers will keep you guessing (Kate Morgan, By Death series), and her romantic comedies will keep you giggling (*It's a Dog's Life*, a stand-alone novella; and the Broken Protocols series, starring Charming Marvin, the cat).

Dale honors the stories that come to her—and some of them are crazy, break all the rules and cross multiple genres!

To go with her fiction, she also writes nonfiction in many different fields, with books available on résumé writing, companion gardening, and the US mortgage system. All her books are available in print and ebook format.

Connect with Dale Mayer Online

Dale's Website – www.dalemayer.com

Twitter – @DaleMayer

Facebook – facebook.com/DaleMayer.author

BookBub – bookbub.com/authors/dale-mayer

Also by Dale Mayer

Published Adult Books:

Shadow Recon
Magnus, Book 1

Bullard's Battle
Ryland's Reach, Book 1
Cain's Cross, Book 2
Eton's Escape, Book 3
Garret's Gambit, Book 4
Kano's Keep, Book 5
Fallon's Flaw, Book 6
Quinn's Quest, Book 7
Bullard's Beauty, Book 8
Bullard's Best, Book 9
Bullard's Battle, Books 1–2
Bullard's Battle, Books 3–4
Bullard's Battle, Books 5–6
Bullard's Battle, Books 7–8

Terkel's Team
Damon's Deal, Book 1
Wade's War, Book 2
Gage's Goal, Book 3
Calum's Contact, Book 4
Rick's Road, Book 5

Kate Morgan

Simon Says… Hide, Book 1
Simon Says… Jump, Book 2
Simon Says… Ride, Book 3
Simon Says… Scream, Book 4
Simon Says… Run, Book 5

Hathaway House

Aaron, Book 1
Brock, Book 2
Cole, Book 3
Denton, Book 4
Elliot, Book 5
Finn, Book 6
Gregory, Book 7
Heath, Book 8
Iain, Book 9
Jaden, Book 10
Keith, Book 11
Lance, Book 12
Melissa, Book 13
Nash, Book 14
Owen, Book 15
Percy, Book 16
Quinton, Book 17
Hathaway House, Books 1–3
Hathaway House, Books 4–6
Hathaway House, Books 7–9

The K9 Files

Ethan, Book 1
Pierce, Book 2

Zane, Book 3
Blaze, Book 4
Lucas, Book 5
Parker, Book 6
Carter, Book 7
Weston, Book 8
Greyson, Book 9
Rowan, Book 10
Caleb, Book 11
Kurt, Book 12
Tucker, Book 13
Harley, Book 14
Kyron, Book 15
Jenner, Book 16
The K9 Files, Books 1–2
The K9 Files, Books 3–4
The K9 Files, Books 5–6
The K9 Files, Books 7–8
The K9 Files, Books 9–10
The K9 Files, Books 11–12

Lovely Lethal Gardens
Arsenic in the Azaleas, Book 1
Bones in the Begonias, Book 2
Corpse in the Carnations, Book 3
Daggers in the Dahlias, Book 4
Evidence in the Echinacea, Book 5
Footprints in the Ferns, Book 6
Gun in the Gardenias, Book 7
Handcuffs in the Heather, Book 8
Ice Pick in the Ivy, Book 9
Jewels in the Juniper, Book 10

Killer in the Kiwis, Book 11
Lifeless in the Lilies, Book 12
Murder in the Marigolds, Book 13
Nabbed in the Nasturtiums, Book 14
Offed in the Orchids, Book 15
Poison in the Pansies, Book 16
Quarry in the Quince, Book 17
Revenge in the Roses, Book 18
Lovely Lethal Gardens, Books 1–2
Lovely Lethal Gardens, Books 3–4
Lovely Lethal Gardens, Books 5–6
Lovely Lethal Gardens, Books 7–8
Lovely Lethal Gardens, Books 9–10

Psychic Vision Series
Tuesday's Child
Hide 'n Go Seek
Maddy's Floor
Garden of Sorrow
Knock Knock...
Rare Find
Eyes to the Soul
Now You See Her
Shattered
Into the Abyss
Seeds of Malice
Eye of the Falcon
Itsy-Bitsy Spider
Unmasked
Deep Beneath
From the Ashes
Stroke of Death

Ice Maiden
Snap, Crackle...
What If...
Talking Bones
Psychic Visions Books 1–3
Psychic Visions Books 4–6
Psychic Visions Books 7–9

By Death Series
Touched by Death
Haunted by Death
Chilled by Death
By Death Books 1–3

Broken Protocols – Romantic Comedy Series
Cat's Meow
Cat's Pajamas
Cat's Cradle
Cat's Claus
Broken Protocols 1-4

Broken and... Mending
Skin
Scars
Scales (of Justice)
Broken but... Mending 1-3

Glory
Genesis
Tori
Celeste
Glory Trilogy

Biker Blues

Morgan: Biker Blues, Volume 1
Cash: Biker Blues, Volume 2

SEALs of Honor

Mason: SEALs of Honor, Book 1
Hawk: SEALs of Honor, Book 2
Dane: SEALs of Honor, Book 3
Swede: SEALs of Honor, Book 4
Shadow: SEALs of Honor, Book 5
Cooper: SEALs of Honor, Book 6
Markus: SEALs of Honor, Book 7
Evan: SEALs of Honor, Book 8
Mason's Wish: SEALs of Honor, Book 9
Chase: SEALs of Honor, Book 10
Brett: SEALs of Honor, Book 11
Devlin: SEALs of Honor, Book 12
Easton: SEALs of Honor, Book 13
Ryder: SEALs of Honor, Book 14
Macklin: SEALs of Honor, Book 15
Corey: SEALs of Honor, Book 16
Warrick: SEALs of Honor, Book 17
Tanner: SEALs of Honor, Book 18
Jackson: SEALs of Honor, Book 19
Kanen: SEALs of Honor, Book 20
Nelson: SEALs of Honor, Book 21
Taylor: SEALs of Honor, Book 22
Colton: SEALs of Honor, Book 23
Troy: SEALs of Honor, Book 24
Axel: SEALs of Honor, Book 25
Baylor: SEALs of Honor, Book 26
Hudson: SEALs of Honor, Book 27

Lachlan: SEALs of Honor, Book 28
Paxton: SEALs of Honor, Book 29
SEALs of Honor, Books 1–3
SEALs of Honor, Books 4–6
SEALs of Honor, Books 7–10
SEALs of Honor, Books 11–13
SEALs of Honor, Books 14–16
SEALs of Honor, Books 17–19
SEALs of Honor, Books 20–22
SEALs of Honor, Books 23–25

Heroes for Hire

Levi's Legend: Heroes for Hire, Book 1
Stone's Surrender: Heroes for Hire, Book 2
Merk's Mistake: Heroes for Hire, Book 3
Rhodes's Reward: Heroes for Hire, Book 4
Flynn's Firecracker: Heroes for Hire, Book 5
Logan's Light: Heroes for Hire, Book 6
Harrison's Heart: Heroes for Hire, Book 7
Saul's Sweetheart: Heroes for Hire, Book 8
Dakota's Delight: Heroes for Hire, Book 9
Tyson's Treasure: Heroes for Hire, Book 10
Jace's Jewel: Heroes for Hire, Book 11
Rory's Rose: Heroes for Hire, Book 12
Brandon's Bliss: Heroes for Hire, Book 13
Liam's Lily: Heroes for Hire, Book 14
North's Nikki: Heroes for Hire, Book 15
Anders's Angel: Heroes for Hire, Book 16
Reyes's Raina: Heroes for Hire, Book 17
Dezi's Diamond: Heroes for Hire, Book 18
Vince's Vixen: Heroes for Hire, Book 19
Ice's Icing: Heroes for Hire, Book 20

Johan's Joy: Heroes for Hire, Book 21
Galen's Gemma: Heroes for Hire, Book 22
Zack's Zest: Heroes for Hire, Book 23
Bonaparte's Belle: Heroes for Hire, Book 24
Noah's Nemesis: Heroes for Hire, Book 25
Tomas's Trials: Heroes for Hire, Book 26
Heroes for Hire, Books 1–3
Heroes for Hire, Books 4–6
Heroes for Hire, Books 7–9
Heroes for Hire, Books 10–12
Heroes for Hire, Books 13–15
Heroes for Hire, Books 16–18
Heroes for Hire, Books 19–21
Heroes for Hire, Books 22–24

SEALs of Steel
Badger: SEALs of Steel, Book 1
Erick: SEALs of Steel, Book 2
Cade: SEALs of Steel, Book 3
Talon: SEALs of Steel, Book 4
Laszlo: SEALs of Steel, Book 5
Geir: SEALs of Steel, Book 6
Jager: SEALs of Steel, Book 7
The Final Reveal: SEALs of Steel, Book 8
SEALs of Steel, Books 1–4
SEALs of Steel, Books 5–8
SEALs of Steel, Books 1–8

The Mavericks
Kerrick, Book 1
Griffin, Book 2
Jax, Book 3

Beau, Book 4
Asher, Book 5
Ryker, Book 6
Miles, Book 7
Nico, Book 8
Keane, Book 9
Lennox, Book 10
Gavin, Book 11
Shane, Book 12
Diesel, Book 13
Jerricho, Book 14
Killian, Book 15
Hatch, Book 16
Corbin, Book 17
The Mavericks, Books 1–2
The Mavericks, Books 3–4
The Mavericks, Books 5–6
The Mavericks, Books 7–8
The Mavericks, Books 9–10
The Mavericks, Books 11–12

Collections
Dare to Be You...
Dare to Love...
Dare to be Strong...
RomanceX3

Standalone Novellas
It's a Dog's Life
Riana's Revenge
Second Chances

Published Young Adult Books:

Family Blood Ties Series
Vampire in Denial
Vampire in Distress
Vampire in Design
Vampire in Deceit
Vampire in Defiance
Vampire in Conflict
Vampire in Chaos
Vampire in Crisis
Vampire in Control
Vampire in Charge
Family Blood Ties Set 1–3
Family Blood Ties Set 1–5
Family Blood Ties Set 4–6
Family Blood Ties Set 7–9
Sian's Solution, A Family Blood Ties Series Prequel
  Novelette

Design series
Dangerous Designs
Deadly Designs
Darkest Designs
Design Series Trilogy

Standalone
In Cassie's Corner
Gem Stone (a Gemma Stone Mystery)
Time Thieves

Published Non-Fiction Books:

Career Essentials

Career Essentials: The Résumé
Career Essentials: The Cover Letter
Career Essentials: The Interview
Career Essentials: 3 in 1

.